RAY OF

LIGHT

(Ray Series #1)

E. L. TODD

6/14/17 × NA

Fallen Publishing
Ray of Light
Editing Services provided by Final-Edits.com
Copyright © 2017 by E. L. Todd☐All Rights Reserved

Chapter One

Rae

"You're such a piece of shit. Shut your ass and pick up after yourself." I kicked his pile of clothes aside, hooking his boxers on the tip of my running shoes. An assortment of dirty clothes was all over the laundry room. I couldn't even walk through it without tripping over something disgusting.

Rex raised both of his hands in the air. "Dude, chill."

"I will not chill." I stomped my feet just like a child. "And I'm not a dude."

"Really?" He cocked his head to the side the way he always did just before he said something smartass. "You fooled me."

I kicked his boxers at him. "Ugh."

"Is that supposed to gross me out?" he asked. "They're mine."

"They should gross you out. They smell like ass."

"Your face smells like ass."

Safari stood in the hallway with his leash in his mouth. It dangled to the hardwood floor. He sat there patiently and waited for his afternoon run through the park. He was a German Shepherd and an excellent dog. The argument didn't faze him at all. He just stood there.

Rex was driving me up the wall. I wanted to murder him in cold blood and not even hide that knowledge from the police. I wanted all the glory for getting rid of this annoying bitch. "You're lucky I'm letting you crash with me until your business picks up. The least you can do is not be a pig."

"How can I when you hold that over my head every other second?" Rex met my fury with his own. He was a formidable opponent when it came to arguing. He knew me well enough to combat anything I said and turn it around on me. He had dark hair that was almost black, and his tall stature dwarfed mine.

"I only hold it over your head when you tear my home apart. Just clean up after yourself. Shit, are you five?"

"I was gonna clean it up but I got caught up—"

"Cut the crap. We both know you weren't going to do it. Now start." I walked around him because I was sick of this argument. I felt like I had a twenty-eight-year-old child living in my apartment.

"You need to get laid, Rae." Rex scooped up his dirty laundry and tossed it in the hamper. "Or you need to wait for your period to pass before you start screaming at everybody."

"Last time I checked, you were the only person I screamed at."

"Well, take me off your list." He grabbed another pair of his boxers and threw them right at my face.

"Ugh." I yanked them off and threw them on the ground. "I hate you."

"Feeling is mutual."

"No, I actually hate you."

"What a coincidence." He headed back to his room, his shoulders tense in rage.

"Where the hell are you going?"

"To my room, nimrod."

"Do your damn laundry! What did we just talk about?"

"I'll wait until you're out." He slammed the door behind him with his foot.

I stared at the closed door and sighed, feeling a mix of emotions burn a hole right through me. Rex was the brother from hell. He was ungrateful for everything I did for him, and he made me a prisoner in my own home. Every day when I came home from work, the kitchen was massacred from all the protein shakes, food, and beer he inhaled all day. I was constantly cleaning up after him just so I would have a hospitable environment.

Safari tilted his head as he looked up at me, the leash still in his mouth. His ears bent down and he released a quiet whine.

"I know," I whispered. "I hate him too."

***

My dog was my personal trainer.

He yanked me down the path even when I wanted to go slow. He was so strong that he pulled me along. Sometimes I thought he was walking me and not the other way around.

I jogged behind him and tried to keep up. "Safari, slow down."

He kept running at full speed.

I kept my pace even though there was a stitch in my side. I was breathing through my mouth the entire time because I was desperate for air. My dog kept me in great shape and constantly reminded me how lazy I was at the same time.

Other joggers passed us through the park, and Safari didn't sniff their butts or interrupt them. He didn't even bark because I trained him so well. He minded his own business and did what he was supposed to.

Except slow the hell down.

This was the only exercise he got all day, and he didn't take that for granted. He cherished every single moment, using his powerful legs to give him enough speed to feel the wind move through his fur. He was running even faster now.

And I was about to die.

"Whoa, slow down." I dug my heels into the concrete and pulled on the leash.

Safari stopped, but instead of slowing down, he turned around and grabbed the leash with his mouth. Then he ripped it out of my hand violently.

"Safari!"

He sprinted at full speed, the leash still dangling in his mouth.

Why was everyone screwing me over today?

I chased after Safari, running as fast as I could, but since we'd already done a few miles, my legs were fatigued. "Safari, get back here now!"

He ran far ahead and passed other joggers headed my way. Without sniffing at the other dogs he came across, he kept going. It wasn't clear what he was so desperate to get to.

"Safari!"

He finally stopped running and switched to a brisk walk. He was headed right to a man running way ahead. With his leash still in his mouth, he ran right up to the man, almost like he knew him.

The man stopped jogging and looked down at Safari. Instead of frowning, he smiled. "Hey, who are you?"

I stopped running because my legs couldn't carry me anymore. Besides, Safari seemed to finally be stationary. Since I was so focused on getting Safari back, I hadn't noticed the man he approached. And now that I took a good look at him, I realized something.

He was hooooot.

Like, damn.

He was over six feet tall. Since I was taller than the average woman, about five nine, tall men were my preference. He was at least three inches taller than me, which was perfect.

On top of that, he was nicely built. He had large shoulders rounded with muscle. He wore a short-sleeve shirt, and the definition of his biceps and forearms was noticeable. I could even see the web of veins on his hands.

Maybe Safari taking off wasn't such a bad thing...

His shirt fit snug against his chest, showing the outline of his pectoral muscles. It was loose around his waist, and the ratio between his waist and shoulders was perfect. His legs were muscular and toned as well.

So pretty.

And his face was the best part. He had short dark brown hair with green eyes. They sparkled under the sunlight, like emeralds that I wanted to hoard. His face was traditionally handsome with nice cheekbones and full lips. The scruff along his chin and jaw was a turn-on. I preferred a little facial hair over the clean look.

Maybe today was about to get a lot better.

He kneeled down and scratched Safari behind the ears. "You want me to take you on a walk?" he asked with a chuckle. His immediate affection toward a random dog told me he was an animal lover.

Even better.

I put my hands on my hips and breathed through the ache in my side. "I'm so sorry. Safari is a bit wild sometimes."

He looked up at me, and the second he did, his smile stretched from ear-to-ear. He had nice teeth, the kind you would see on a model. His eyes were the best part. They were pretty to look at, but they held a mysterious energy. They changed as they examined me, but I couldn't figure out what the look meant. "Safari? The name suits him."

"A little too well, actually."

He patted Safari on the head before he rose to his full height. His earbuds were dangling from around his neck, and his t-shirt had the Seahawks logo on it. Judging by his lean build, he was an active runner. But judging by the nice size of his muscles, he was also a frequent visitor to the weight room. "There's no need for an apology. Your dog is friendly."

"He is." I gave Safari a look that said he was in trouble. "Too friendly."

His ears bent down.

The man chuckled. "How can you be mad at this guy? He's just an adventurer."

"You could have been a dognapper."

"A dognapper?" he asked. "Who would steal a dog?"

"I don't know...but it could happen."

He grabbed the leash from Safari's mouth then handed it over. "Sorry, boy. Maybe I can give you a walk some other time."

I took the leash from him, and when our hands were in contact, I noticed the heat radiating from his body. It was nice. Waking up in his arms would be a great way to start a rainy morning. "Sorry again. We didn't mean to interrupt your run."

"It's okay," he said. "I was pretty bored anyway."

When I realized I was fidgeting with Safari's leash, I forced myself to stop. Handsome men didn't make me uneasy very often. My confidence was always high no matter how hot they were. But this guy got under my skin a little bit.

"I'm Ryker, by the way."

Even his name was hot. I'd never heard that one before. "Rae."

"Rae." He repeated the name like he was trying to memorize it. "Ray of light?"

"I think so."

"You don't know?" he asked.

Unfortunately, no. "Thanks for being so nice to my dog. I'll let you get back to your jog."

He eyed me like I hadn't said anything. "Want to walk to Pike Place Market? It's just a block over."

Was this beautiful man asking me out? I hid my squeal and acted cool. "Sure. I have a feeling Safari will just run after you again if I try to walk away."

"I must smell." He realized what he said when it was too late. "I mean, I must smell good."

I pressed my lips tightly together and tried not to laugh.

Ryker shrugged and laughed all the same. "Okay...that came out wrong."

I couldn't hold back my laughter. "Yeah...a little."

***

"How old is Safari?" Ryker stuffed his earbuds into his pocket and walked beside me through the market.

"Five."

"He's a good-looking dog."

"Thank you. He's my best friend."

"Really?" he asked.

"Well, I have two human best friends too. If they knew Safari was my best best friend, they would get jealous...so I don't mention it."

Ryker smiled. It was the kind of look that turned all women into putty. My ovaries screamed from deep inside my body, needing his perfect genes to make the cutest baby in the world. "Your secret is safe with me."

"Thank you. Do you have a dog?"

"No, not yet. Maybe soon."

"Start with a plant," I said. "They're easier to take care of."

"Safari doesn't seem so bad...when he's not running away from you."

I laughed at the memory. "He's never done that before. It was really strange."

"Like I said, I smell." He smiled again, his eyes glowing as he did.

I chuckled. I loved his sense of humor. He was extremely good-looking but didn't take himself seriously. Humility was another quality I liked in a man. "Seahawks fan?"

"Their number one fan."

"Really?"

"You aren't?" he asked in surprise.

"I admire their fan base and think it's great so many people get involved, but no, they aren't my favorite team."

He took an exaggerated step off to the side. "This is awkward..."

I kept my hand on Safari's leash and tried not to smile. "We can still be friends, right?"

He kept his distance. "I don't know..."

"Come on, let's put our differences aside."

"They're pretty big differences."

"People have overcome worse."

He nodded in agreement. "Okay…I guess that's true." He came back to my side and kept walking. "I'll be your friend."

"Thanks."

He put his hands in his pockets and came closer to me, his arm brushing against my shoulder every few seconds. "Live here your whole life?"

"Yep. You?"

"I just moved here a few weeks ago."

"Oh, really?" I asked. "From where?"

"Manhattan."

"That's a far move."

"And an annoying one."

"What brings you here?"

"I'm starting a new job." He didn't sound too enthused by the prospect. He was more passionate about the Seahawks a second ago.

"What line of work are you in?"

"I'm taking over the family business." He brushed over it quickly like he didn't want to talk about it too much. "Nothing too interesting. But I wish I'd become a dog trainer instead. Apparently, I have a knack for it."

"Safari may like you, but that doesn't mean you could train him. He's stubborn sometimes."

"I find that hard to believe."

"He takes up the whole bed every night. And he's a blanket hogger."

Ryker grinned from ear-to-ear. "You sleep with him every night?"

"Pretty much."

"Hmm...that must mean you don't have a boyfriend."

I kept my eyes on Safari and tried not to react visibly. The schoolgirl inside me wanted to smile and giggle. My cheeks wanted to blush beet red. Somehow, I managed to come off pleased but not obsessive. "No, I don't."

"Interesting."

"I dumped my last boyfriend because he became a Seahawk fan though."

"Oh no," he said with a cringe. "Looks like I don't stand a chance then."

I couldn't disagree more.

My phone vibrated in my pocket, so I discreetly checked it. It was a text message from Cameron.

I'll pick you up at seven? Is that okay? I can't wait to see you. I've been thinking about this date all week.

My eyes widened to orbs, and I quickly shoved my phone back into my pocket. Goddammit, I forgot about that date. Jessie arranged it for me even though I didn't want to go on it to begin with.

"Everything alright?" Ryker asked.

"Yeah, groovy." Was I a hippie now?

We continued walking through the market and making small talk. I learned Ryker was a big sports fan. Anything that involved a ball or a puck had his attention. He seemed like a sports guy so I wasn't surprised.

He checked the watch on his wrist. "It's getting late, and I'm done with my cardio for the day."

"Yeah." I had to get ready for a stupid date.

"My apartment is just a block over." He stopped walking and faced me head-on. His emerald eyes bore into mine, having that cutting edge again. They were full of mystery but also a lot more. It would be so easy to fall into those eyes and never come back up for air. "Why don't the two of you come over?"

That didn't sound like a date. It sounded like an invitation to sex. One-night stands weren't new to me, but I didn't do them very often. Judging by Ryker's looks and moves, he had no problem landing a fuck buddy in thirty minutes. He probably did it all the time.

I was really into him, and sharing a bed with a hunky man like him for the night sounded like a treat I desperately needed. We hadn't kissed, but I could tell it would be pretty damn fantastic.

Just when I was about to say yes, I realized something. "Actually, I can't." I sighed in irritation because I was missing out on sex with a hot guy because of Jessie.

"Oh." He kept the displeasure off his face, but he couldn't keep it out of his eyes. "Have plans?"

"Uh, I have a date." Cameron was a nice guy and good-looking, but he was so forward that it drove me crazy. He was always telling me how pretty I was, and he laughed at every joke even if it wasn't funny. There was just no mystery there. But I couldn't blow off a date at the last minute just because I met someone better. And I definitely couldn't have sex with one guy then go on a date with another guy two hours later. One-night stands were fine, but if I did that, I'd be a straight-up slut.

"Bad timing, I guess."

I waited for him to ask me out for another time, perhaps tomorrow or this weekend.

But he didn't. "It was nice meeting you, Rae."

That was it? We couldn't go out for a drink some other time? "You too, Ryker. Maybe we can go out some other time." Even though I wanted to see him again, I kept my eagerness back. Being too forward was a turnoff. I quickly learned that from Cameron.

"Maybe." He patted Safari on the head. "See you around, boy." He gave me a final look before he walked off and headed into the crowd.

I stood there with the leash in my hand, totally bummed out that I missed out on something great. He seemed to like me, so why didn't he ask me out? It was either now or never?

But if he wasn't willing to see me some other time, then he probably wasn't worth my time anyway. I was okay with being single, unlike most women, but I was tired of falling for all the selfish jerks and not caring about the sweet, good ones.

What was up with that?

Chapter Two

Rae

Cameron stared at me for an entire minute without blinking. His eyes were glued to mine, and not in a romantic, intense way. In a straight up creepy way. "You're so pretty."

I gripped the menu just so I had something to do. "Thank you." I looked down at the selections even though I knew what I was going to order. Perhaps if I ignored him long enough, he would stop staring at me like I was a hidden treasure. The heat from his gaze still burned my skin, so I looked up.

"You must get hit on all the time."

Getting a compliment was always nice, but this excessive infatuation was getting annoying. He never had anything to say unless he was commenting on my appearance. "Uh, I wouldn't say that."

"You're just being humble." He grabbed the menu but didn't look at it. His eyes were reserved for me.

What the hell was Jessie thinking setting me up with him? "Do you like being a firefighter? From what I hear, it sounds pretty thrilling." Maybe a change of subject would make this night a little less uncomfortable.

"It can be," he said. "But most of the time, we just sit around in the firehouse. Due to the rain, we don't have many fires."

"But firefighters do other stuff too, right?"

"Yeah. We get called out to accidents from time to time. But even that is rare."

I had a feeling the topic had been exhausted but I wanted to keep it going so it wouldn't return to me. "Do you ever drive the fire truck?"

"Sometimes."

"That must be a wild ride."

"Yeah," he said. "I like turning on the lights and speeding through all the intersections. Wish I could do that all the time."

"Don't we all," I said with a fake chuckle.

"Did you know the fire truck doesn't require a key?"

I shook my head.

"You just press a button on the dashboard."

"Really?" I asked. "Doesn't that mean someone could steal it?"

He grinned. "Don't tell anyone I told you that."

When he wasn't being obsessive, he was actually interesting. Instead of focusing on me, he put the spotlight on himself and revealed more of his depth. "I'll keep your secret."

The waiter came to our table and took our drink order. I ordered a glass of wine but wished I could get a few shots instead. The dating game was exhausting after a while. Now when I went on a date, I prepared for the worst rather than the best. When we placed our dinner order, Cameron ordered for both of us.

"My beautiful date will have the chicken piccata."

Ugh.

"I'll put the order in for you, sir." The waiter took the menus then attended to the other tables.

How long would it take him to bring the wine?

I needed wine—now.

"Did you ever consider modeling?" Cameron asked without preamble. He just blurted it out like we had just been talking about it.

"No..." I got my master's in chemistry and played college basketball. If I had it my way, I would only wear jeans and a hoodie. I grew up a tomboy, and I will always be a tomboy deep down inside. "Cameron, I mean this in the best way possible, but could you be a little less forward?" Saying that would make the evening awkward, but whatever, it already was awkward.

"Forward?" he asked. "What do you mean?"

"It's just...when you constantly comment on my appearance, it makes me a little uncomfortable."

"Oh." A blank look was on his face, like he had no idea what I was referring to.

"You know, saying I'm pretty and stuff like that."

"Well...I think you're pretty," he said with a shrug. "Don't girls like stuff like that?"

"Of course," I said. "But everything in moderation, right?"

He leaned back in his chair and had a sour look on his face. "I didn't realize it made you uncomfortable."

"I guess I'm a little self-conscious about my appearance."

"Why?" he blurted. "You're a perfect ten."

I was liking this less and less. "Not once have you shown any interest in me personally. You don't care about my interests, my hobbies, or anything else. Maybe you're looking for a relationship based on physical appearance but I'm not."

He rolled his eyes from across the table.

"I'm sorry," I said sarcastically. "Am I annoying you?"

"I'm just trying to be a nice guy, and then you snap at me."

"I didn't snap. I just asked you to stop repeating yourself like a damn parrot."

His eyes narrowed on my face. They smoldered like coals coming to a blaze. "Fine. You want me to tell you that you're ugly?"

"Now you're just acting like a child."

"And you're being rude."

"Me?" I asked incredulously. "How would you feel if I kept saying how hot you were all the time?"

He grinned like a fool.

"Never mind," I said quickly.

"Look, I'm just really attracted to you. Is it that big of a deal?"

I tried to remember his compliments came from a good place. He didn't comment on my chest or anything else perverse, so it really wasn't that bad. Perhaps his words bothered me because I wasn't attracted to him in the same way. I wondered what my reaction would have been if Ryker said all of that to me. I had a feeling it would be much different. "You're right. I apologize."

"And I accept your apology."

"Great." I fidgeted with my hands in my lap and felt the tension settle in the room. It burned the back of my neck and made me feel a constant twinge of anxiety.

Where were those drinks?

The waiter finally brought my wine and his beer. I snatched it from him quickly and took a long drink, needing a buzz to get through the rest of the night. Now I wish I'd just taken Ryker's offer and joined him in his apartment. The sex would have been great, and I would be satisfied right now.

***

Cameron walked me to my door, and before I could even say goodnight or reach for my keys, he was all over me. He pushed me against the door and crushed his mouth to mine. When he kissed me, it wasn't in an aggressive or sexy way. His tongue practically licked my face before it stuffed itself inside my mouth.

I gasped for air. "What are you doing?"

"What does it look like I'm doing?" He shoved his tongue into my mouth again, and slobber actually dripped down my chin. How he transferred so much saliva into my mouth that quickly was beyond my understanding.

I pushed him away then wiped my mouth. "Thank you for dinner. I'm turning in for the night."

Cameron didn't mask his disappointment. "How about I join you?"

Did he just invite himself into my apartment? "I don't think that's a good idea. Good night." I slipped my key in the door. For the first time in my life, I was grateful my brother was living with me. If I needed help, he was there.

"Come on." Cameron came closer to me. "What can I do to change your mind?"

"Nothing. My brother is here."

"He lives with you?" he asked in surprise.

"Yeah. And he's very protective of me, so you should go."

He stepped back slightly. "You can always come to my place."

Would this date just end? "I have to get up early in the morning. Good night, Cameron." I finally got the door open and quickly shut it behind me. After the door was locked and the chain was hooked in place, I breathed a sigh of relief.

That's when I noticed the sound of moaning coming from the living room.

I walked in and saw Rex sitting on the couch watching porn. He was fully clothed, and his arms were over the back of the couch. The scene was right on my TV screen. "What the hell are you doing?"

He flinched when he realized I was there. "What?"

"Why are you so disgusting?"

"It's not like I'm touching myself."

"Then why are you watching it?"

He shrugged. "It's soothing."

I wanted to rip my hair out of my skull and scream at the top of my lungs.

"Besides, I thought you would be gone all night. Didn't you have a date?"

"Yes, but it was terrible." The scene still played on the TV, and both actors were breathing hard and moaning like they were having the best time of their lives. "Can you turn that off now?"

"Why? It's just porn."

"And it's my TV. Watch it in your room."

He rolled his eyes and turned it off. "There. Can you chill out now?"

I threw my purse on the table and didn't retrieve my phone from inside it. I didn't want any further contact for the night. All I wanted to do was go to bed and forget this day ever happened.

***

I was a researcher for COLLECT recycling company. My job was to decrease the amount of waste being deposited into our landfills by creating products that were either recyclable or biodegradable. Environmental science had always been my forte, and to say I was passionate about my job was an understatement.

The first year I started working here, I reduced the amount of waste by five percent. That might not sound like a big number, but over the course of the year, it was thousands of tons of garbage.

Most people didn't think twice about the garbage they put into their waste cans or where it went, but it was a serious problem. I knew I couldn't fix every issue we came across, but I did my best to make a difference.

Right then, I was working on biodegradable food storage packages. Egg cartons, deli meat containers, orange juice jugs, and everything else that Americans bought on a daily basis. If I could figure out a way to make it completely degradable, it would be revolutionary in waste management.

But that wasn't something I would figure out overnight.

Jenny came to my workbench, wearing her white lab coat without her protective goggles. "Did you hear the news?"

I paused the experiment inside the chemical hood and put the specimens down. After I pulled off my nitrogen gloves and tossed them aside, I looked at her. "What news?"

"Mr. Price is retiring."

Mr. Price was the CEO of the company. He built it at a very young age and had run it ever since. He was getting old, and I suspected his health was poor judging by the way he sometimes walked, but I wasn't expecting this. "He is?"

She nodded. "I can't say I'm surprised though. He's pretty old."

Mr. Price was one of the greatest bosses I ever worked for. He was generous and compassionate. Even though I didn't see him often, I loved being in his presence. He was like the father I never had. "That's too bad."

"Yeah."

"How did you find out?"

"They're sending memos to all the departments. My friend in accounting told me."

It would be weird not having Mr. Price around. Who would take over? What would they be like? Would I still have a job? "Is the company being sold?"

"No. But I'm quitting anyway."

"You're quitting?" I took off my goggles. "But you love it here."

"I know," she said with a sigh. "It's going to be hard to leave this place. But I'm not putting up with the playboy that's taking Mr. Price's place."

"Playboy?" I asked.

"His son is taking over the company. From what I hear, he's some rich asshole that's never worked a day in his life. He graduated from Harvard then lived off Daddy's investments until he was asked to step up. There's no way in hell I'm dealing with some jerk like that."

"But you haven't even met him..."

"I've heard enough."

"And would Mr. Price put his son in charge if he didn't think he would be successful?" I was usually the voice of reason between Jenny and me.

"Parents are always blind when it comes to their kids."

"Maybe you should stick around and see how it goes first. If he's really that lazy, he probably won't change anything."

"Or he'll cut all our salaries so he pockets more of the dough."

"Again...you're conjecturing here."

She raised both hands in frustration. "It's never going to be the same. Everything here was so great, and I'm not willing to see it change."

"Just don't be hasty. Give it a chance before you submit your resignation. And if not, at least wait until you find another job."

She crossed her arms over her chest.

"Jenny, everything will be fine. Now take a deep breath."

She rolled her eyes but did as I said.

"Let's take it one day at a time—together."

Chapter Three

Rae

I found the girls sitting at a table in the bar. "I have a bone to pick with you."

Jessie's face lit up when she saw me, and the alcohol she'd consumed had turned her cheeks red. "Look who's here! Ray of light!"

I dropped into the chair and glared at her.

"How was your date?" Kayden asked, completely oblivious to my pissed look.

Jessie threw her hands in the air like it was time to party. "You're welcome, girl. I bet he rocked your world good."

Jessie was only fun when she was drunk when I was also drunk. "Cameron was terrible. How could you set me up with him?"

"Terrible?" Jessie asked. "What are you talking about?"

I started to imitate him. "You're so beautiful. Do you know how pretty you are? Man, you're gorgeous." I rolled my eyes so hard it actually hurt the front of my face a little bit. "Does he know how to say anything else?"

Kayden held a pink cosmo in her hand. "Sounds sweet to me."

"It was sweet—when he said it the first time. But then he kept repeating it over and over. I wanted to shove crackers down his throat to make it stop."

Jessie laughed and bit the olive off her toothpick. "There are worse things."

"He was so desperate," I said. "And then when I asked him to stop, he turned it into an ordeal—"

Jessie raised her hand to silence me. "You're so picky when it comes to guys. If you just had an open mind, maybe you'd find someone you really like. If you keep cutting them out every time they do one little thing, you're going to die alone."

"I haven't even gotten to the worst part yet." I crossed my arms over my chest.

"Ooh...this sounds good." Kayden downed the rest of her drink.

"When we got to my door, he shoved me against it and decided to play Operation with his tongue. He stuck his tongue everywhere, and it even went up my nose."

Kayden cringed. "Eww!"

"Gross," Jessie said.

"Slobber actually dripped off my chin and fell on the floor. I heard it splash." It was the worst make out session I ever had, and I'd been to sixth grade camp. "He was the worst kisser ever, and he acted like it was some of his best stuff. I don't care if he's a hot firefighter. That guy is one cleverly disguised freak."

"Wow..." Jessie abandoned her drink, clearly not thirsty anymore. "Damn, that does sound bad."

Kayden shivered. "So gross."

"So, I'm not seeing him again." I shot them both a glare. "And it's not because I'm picky."

"We hear ya," Jessie said.

"We accept your decision," Kayden said.

I massaged the back of my neck because I felt a kink coming on. "So, what's new with you guys?"

"I heard COLLECT is getting a new show runner," Jessie said.

"What?" I blurted. "How did you know about that?"

"I read it in the paper. And I have to say, the new guy is H-O-T."

"He is?" Jenny never mentioned that.

"Yeah," Jessie said. "He looked hot in the photograph. At least you'll have someone pretty to take orders from."

"I just hope he's not as terrible as my coworker made it sound," I said.

Jessie shrugged. "It didn't really say anything in the article, but from what I've learned, anyone who grows up with money is usually a bit of a jerk. Self-made billionaires are the humble ones."

"True," Kayden said. Her long, blonde hair was in big curls and trailed down over one shoulder. Her sparkling blue eyes made her look like a porcelain doll.

"When does he officially start working?" Jessie asked.

I shrugged. "Honestly, I don't know. In the research lab, we don't usually deal with anyone besides each other. So, whether he's good or bad, I probably won't have to deal with him much."

"Unless you're screwing," Jessie said.

I shot her a glare. "I would never sleep with my boss—no matter how good-looking he was."

"I would," Jessie said. "That's how hot this guy is."

"I need to see him for myself," Kayden said. "I don't get too many lookers in the library."

"Because it's the library," Jessie jabbed. "Get out and live a little."

Kayden raised her empty glass. "Thank you very much."

***

When I came home from work, Zeke and Rex were there.

"I can't believe he's back in town." Zeke's voice came from the living room. "We haven't seen that guy in...at least ten years."

"I know, right?" Rex said. "The second he graduated, he took off. Wanted to get as far away from this place as possible."

"What are you guys talking about?" I set my purse on the counter then grabbed a beer from the fridge.

"Ugh," Rex said. "The monster is here."

"The monster was about to bring you another beer, but forget it now."

Rex quickly changed his mind. "I mean, the greatest little sister ever is here." He made his voice high-pitched. "Yay."

"Better." I walked into the living room and handed him the bottle.

Zeke's eyes followed my every movement. "Hey, Rae. How's it going?"

"Good."

"How'd that date go?" Zeke took a drink of his beer.

"Horrible." I sat on the couch beside him and relaxed into the cushions. In the lab, I was on my feet all day long. Whenever I sat down, my ass actually felt happy.

"That bad?" Zeke was technically my brother's friend, but he was my friend too.

"He spit in my mouth. Let's put it that way." I was still brushing my teeth vigorously to get all that spit out of my mouth.

Rex's face contorted into a look I'd never seen before. He looked disgusted but curious at the same time. "You're saying he literally spit in your mouth?"

"Pretty much." I took a long drink of the beer to get rid of the taste that still lingered far behind.

"How would that even happen?" Zeke asked. "I mean, you just stood there with your mouth open and let him?"

"Yeah?" Rex asked. "Was it like a game of darts?"

"No!" Their imagination always took dangerous roads. "At the end of the date, he went for the good night kiss and it turned into him drowning me with his mouth. God, it was disgusting."

"So, you just pushed him off, and that was it?" Zeke asked.

"He wanted to come inside and screw," I said. "But I told him to take a hike. If he kisses like that, imagine how he is in bed." I shivered at the thought.

"I wonder why Jessie set you up with him?" Zeke asked.

"I don't have a damn clue," I said. "I'm not sure if she even had a conversation with him—ever. He probably just told her he thought I was cute and she played cupid."

"Well, she should keep her day job," Rex said. "She's not very good at matchmaking."

I turned to Zeke. He was my brother's best friend, so he understood just how annoying Rex was. "When I came home, Rex was watching porn in the living room. Can you believe that?"

Zeke gave Rex a disgusted look. "You were beating off even though you knew your sister was coming home?"

"Hell no," Rex said. "I was just watching it. You know, for the surround sound."

"Oh." Zeke nodded in understanding. "Now I get it."

"What?" I was about to take a drink of my beer but stopped. "You get it?"

"It doesn't sound the same on a computer," Zeke said. "If you have the right speakers, you really get the full effect."

Men were gross.

"Right?" Rex said. "You watch it on your TV too?"

"When I'm single," Zeke said.

"Exactly," Rex said. "The TV is better."

"But it's my TV," I argued. "Don't forget you live with me right now."

"How could I?" He shot me a glare before he took a drink of his beer.

"Zeke, why don't you take him?" I pouted my lips and pleaded with my eyes.

Zeke shook his head. "Hell. No. If I did, we wouldn't be friends anymore."

"Hey." Rex gave him an offended look. "Bros before hoes, dude."

"I'm just being honest," Zeke said. "Would bros lie to each other?"

Rex looked away when he didn't have a comeback.

Zeke turned back to me. "We're going to play ball. You want in?"

"Don't invite her," Rex said. "She's such a pain on the court."

"Am not," I argued. "You just think I'm a pain because I'm better than all of you."

"You foul everyone like crazy," Rex argued.

"No, I don't," I said. "I shove them out of the way just the way LeBron does, but you give me shit for it because I'm a girl."

"I want her to play," Zeke said. "She can be on my team."

"You mean, you can be on my team," I said.

Zeke glared at me. "Hey, if it weren't for me, you wouldn't be playing ball at all."

"See?" Rex said. "I told you my sister is a pain in the ass. I prefer to call her SAID."

This nickname was the stupidest one I'd ever heard. He kept it between us, but it seemed like he was going to include Zeke in the know now.

"SAID?" Zeke asked. "Do I want to know?"

"It means stupid, annoying, irritating, and dumb." Rex tapped his finger against his head like he was being clever.

Zeke bottled his laugh and didn't let it escape because I was sitting right there. He covered his mouth with his lips, but his chest heaved a few times like he was trying to keep it in.

"It's great, huh?" Rex said. "I can get everything out with just a single word. Saves me so much time."

"That's ironic," I said. "Because I have a nickname for you too."

"Yeah?" Rex asked. "Coolest guy in the world? Everyone calls me that so it doesn't really count."

"What is it?" Zeke asked.

"HPOS," I said.

Zeke raised an eyebrow. "What does that mean?"

I gave Rex a triumphant look. "Homeless piece of shit."

***

We walked down the street to the local courts just a few blocks over. School had gotten out long ago so we hoped there weren't any kids hogging it. Otherwise, we'd have to play with them like last time.

Rex tried spinning the ball on his forefinger. "How does Michael Jordan do it?" The ball kept falling over sideways and he had to steady it.

"First off," I said. "He knows how to play basketball. Second of all, he has manly hands. You have little fairy hands."

Rex threw the ball at my shoulder, and he caught it when it bounced back. "Turd."

"Is that supposed to stand for something?" I asked sarcastically.

"Nope," Rex said. "The meaning is implied."

We rounded the corner then reached the courts. They were blocked by a metal fence and were situated between two apartment buildings. I felt bad for whoever lived there.

"A few of my friends are playing with us," Rex said.

"I know." I rolled my eyes. "I've met them all before."

"Well, my buddy from New York is here too. He just moved back. Zeke and I haven't seen him in ages."

I didn't care for his biography. "Is he any good?"

"Definitely," Zeke said. "We played basketball with him in high school."

The air was cold outside and the sky was overcast. It looked like rain but we hoped it didn't. The sweatpants and sweater I wore weren't water-resistant. We'd played in the rain before and it was fine, but I got sick afterward.

"Yo." Rex greeted Toby with a high-five. "What's going on, man?"

"Nothing much," he said. "Just ready to kick your ass."

"Ha." Rex clapped him on the shoulder. "Good one." He turned to the other guy, blocked from my view by Rex's shoulders. "Oh my god, look who's all grown up." He embraced him with a fist bump then stepped back.

When Rex moved out of the way, I got a look at him. My eyes immediately registered his facial features and the bright color of his eyes. His dark hair was short and slightly curly at the ends. His expansive shoulders filled out his t-shirt, and his muscular legs were just the same as they were the other day.

It was Ryker.

When he walked away from me, I thought we would never see each other again. But somehow, our paths had crossed once more. My heart fluttered in my chest and formed wings like a butterfly. Even though he walked away from me without asking me out, I still felt the heat in my core when I looked at him.

"Dude, how've you been?" Rex asked.

"Great," Ryker said. "It's nice to be back home."

Rex tucked the ball under his arm. "You're full of shit."

Ryker smiled when he'd been caught. "Okay. I'm not a big fan of Seattle."

"Then why are you here?" Rex asked.

"Dad needed my help with the business." Without even saying it, it was clear he wanted nothing to do with his job. He was being forced. "And you can't turn your back on family, right?"

"Never." Rex turned my way. "Speaking of which, here's my annoying sister, Rae."

My eyes met his, and an unspoken conversation passed between us. Judging by the slight surprise in his eyes, he never expected to see me again. He didn't look pleased or disappointed.

Ryker recovered from the shock quicker than I did. He stepped closer to me, towering over me with his height. A slight smile was on his lips, along with the scruff that had been there just a few days ago. "It's nice to see you again."

"You too."

"Where's Safari?"

"At home. He'll chase the ball across the court if I bring him."

"Uh...what?" Rex eyed us back and forth. "You know each other?"

"We ran into each other in the park," Ryker said calmly. "Safari wanted to come home with me."

I did too.

Ryker stared hard into my eyes, like he was trying to look for something. "How'd that date go?"

"Terrible."

"Yeah?" he asked. "Was the guy a psychopath?"

"Just a sloppy kisser."

Ryker chuckled then stepped back. "Those are the worst." He turned to Zeke then greeted him. "You've really caked on the muscle, man."

"I got into weight lifting in college." Zeke wasn't as warm to his old friend as I thought he would be. He hardly gave him a handshake before he stepped back. "Let's get the game started."

Ryker raised an eyebrow slightly but quickly brushed it off.

"Alright," Rex said. "I don't care how the teams work out, but I'm not on my sister's team."

"She's playing with us?" Ryker asked in surprise.

The tension suddenly fell on all of us, and it was palpable.

Rex rubbed his temple in irritation. "Man, you shouldn't have said that..."

I crossed my arms over my chest and gave him a venomous glare. "Why is that surprising? Because I'm a woman?"

Ryker knew he said the wrong thing. "No, that's not what I meant."

"Then what did you mean, exactly?"

Zeke took the ball from Rex then dribbled it between his legs. "Rae is the best player out of all of us. So watch yourself."

Ryker played it cool and hid his thoughts behind his eyes. "In that case, I want to be on her team."

Rex leaned toward Ryker and lowered his voice to a whisper. "Good save…"

"Let's play," I said. "I'm done with the chit chat."

***

Ryker was a good ball player like I expected him to be.

But I was better.

I was quicker on the court, and I had more control over the ball. And just like my man, Stephen Curry, I could down those three-pointers with ease. Whenever Rex blocked me, he was forceful. He didn't care about giving me a hard shove or throwing his shoulder in my face. I played hard and so did he. Whenever Zeke was on me, he always kept his distance. He refrained from touching me at all costs. Even though my brother knocked me around, Zeke still treated me like I was fragile. The gentleman inside him just wouldn't die.

By the end of the game, we were thirty points ahead. "And that's how it's done." I made a dramatic bow.

Rex stuck his hand in my hair and messed it up forcefully. "What's the point in winning when you're hideous?" He dribbled the ball and walked to his water bottle near the bench.

Zeke came up to me, sweaty and still out of breath. "Good game." He high-fived me.

"Good game," I said in return. "You're quick on the court."

He put his hands on his hips as he tried to catch his breath. "Not as quick as you."

"Well, nobody is." I flipped my hair and jutted my nose into the air.

Zeke laughed then gave me a playful shove. "Brat."

I shoved him back. "Sore loser."

"Did you ever consider the fact that I might have let you win?"

"Hmm...not really."

"Well, maybe I did. Losing would hurt that ego you carry everywhere you go."

"I think your ego is the one at stake here, so I'll go along with your story to preserve it."

He chuckled then shoved me again. "Loser."

"Let's head to Bill's," Rex said. "I'm thirsty."

"That's a bar," I noted.

"Duh." He rolled his eyes then started walking with Ryker and Tobias.

Zeke stayed by my side and walked with me. "I could use a cold beer right now."

"After exercising?"

"Isn't that the whole point of working out?" he asked. "So you can eat whatever you want?"

"I eat whatever I want regardless."

"You're lucky your physique stays nice on its own."

I laughed. "My physique?"

"What?" he asked. "You don't know what the definition is?"

"It's just a funny way of saying it. And believe me, it doesn't stay nice. My thighs are like the blob. Whenever I take my pants off, I wonder if I should run away from them screaming."

"Since running requires the use of your legs, that'd be pretty difficult to manage."

"I could saw them off. Then you can put them back on." Zeke was a doctor. He'd been running his own practice for a while now.

"I'm not a surgeon," he said. "I'm a dermatologist."

"That's right. You aren't a real doctor." I tried not to smile after I said that last part. Rex and I liked to tease him for this. When he got beet red, it was really funny.

"I am a real doctor."

"Popping zits is a medical treatment?"

He glared at me for a second before a smile started to form. He knew I was trying to get a rise out of him. "What's so special about today?"

Now I was drawing a blank. "What?"

"Today is the day you want to die, right?" He raised his hands like he was about to tickle me to death.

I eyed them with dread and tried to think of an escape plan. "It's funny that you say that—" I took off at a dead run, pushing Rex aside as I tried to get away from Zeke.

Zeke stayed far behind. "Good decision."

***

I didn't want to feel left out, so I ordered a beer like everyone else. Orders of fries and wings were on the way, and the TV showed a sports report about the last Seahawks game.

"Where's your place?" Ryker sat beside Rex, right across from me.

Rex rested his elbows on the table with his eyes glued to the screen. "I have an apartment a few blocks away."

"Eh-hem." I cleared my throat loudly because of the false information he gave.

Ryker eyed me, not sure what the interruption meant.

"He means to say, my apartment." My fingertips touched the frosty glass of the beer. My stomach was aching because I hadn't put food in it for so long. Greasy wings and even greasier fries sounded like the best thing ever made. "He lives with me."

Ryker didn't give him any heat for it. "You like the company?"

"Ugh." Rex rolled his eyes and his head at the same time. It looked like his head was about to fall off. "Hell no. I had to because I'm broke."

I turned to Zeke. "You know, you can take him whenever you want."

"And have him trash my place?" He shook his head slightly. "No, thanks." His dark bark-colored hair contrasted against the fair complexion of his face. He was easy on the eyes, and girls flocked to both him and my brother like geese. I'd been friends with him since I could remember. He was the other brother I never had, the good one.

"Why are you broke?" Ryker asked.

"I bought a bowling alley," Rex said.

Ryker was about to take a drink but stopped himself. "A bowling alley?"

That goddamn bowling alley had been nothing but a pain in the ass. "Rex won the lottery."

"Are you serious?" Ryker asked. "The actual lotto?"

"Yeah," Rex said. "It was a hundred grand."

"And this idiot decided to buy a bowling alley," I said. "It's the worst investment ever. He's barely broken even for the past year. And most importantly, Rex doesn't know anything about bowling. He's never even played."

"Hey, Miss Prissy," Rex snapped. "Why don't you stop being so negative all the time? I don't shove every one of your failures down your throat."

"Uh, yes, you do." What kind of memory did he have?

Rex ignored me and continued talking to Ryker. "The economy has been shit for a while so business hasn't picked up. I keep waiting it out but nothing seems to change. I may have to sell it, and I probably won't get my money back."

Even though my brother pissed me off when he was a pig around the house, brought strange women to the apartment, and insulted me in front of everyone we knew, he always had my back. I knew I needed to be more supportive of this. "Maybe you need to make a few changes."

"Changes?" Rex asked.

"You know, remodel or something."

"But that costs money," he snapped. "In case you were wondering why I'm living with you, it's because I don't have any money."

"I have my savings," I offered. "It can be put to good use."

Zeke looked at me like I just sprouted wings and horns.

Rex's jaw dropped to the surface of the table. "Shut your ass."

"But you know what I think would be really good?" I said. "If you opened a bar. I know they're a lot of work because you have to get the license, but if you had booze and good food to accompany the game, people would really consider it a night out."

Ryker nodded in agreement, his green eyes flashing. "That's not a bad idea."

"And if we slapped a new coat of paint on the outside and told people we were having a re-grand

49

opening, your business would definitely pick up." I learned that in a business class in college. Drawing that kind of attention always increased sales. It was the reason so many fast-food chains remodeled every five years as a rule of thumb.

Zeke nodded in agreement. "Maybe you should have ditched science for marketing."

"Nah," I said. "I like where I am."

"You're a scientist?" Ryker asked in interest.

Anytime he spoke directly to me, I felt my stomach tie up in knots. It was hard to be myself around him because I tensed up anxiously. "My fields of study are environmental chemistry and biology."

He sipped his beer with a look of approval in his eyes. "That's really cool."

Zeke nudged me gently in the side. "Beauty and brains. You don't see that very often."

I smiled at him with gratitude. "Thank you."

"Beauty?" Rex asked. "Anytime I look at Rae, I think of wombat trying to take a shit."

Tobias was about to drink his beer when he stopped and almost knocked the glass over. "Who the hell says stuff like that?"

"It's true," Rex said. "It's the way she does her hair."

"Straight...?" I hardly touched my hair because I was so lazy. When I went out with Jessie and Kayden, I really put time into my appearance, but other than that, it was the path of least resistance. "And remember, I just offered to help you."

"Damn." Rex sighed like he just realized his mistake. "I mean, you're okay."

That was the most I would ever get out of him. "I'll take it."

"This is going to cost a lot of money," Zeke said. "I'll chip in."

"No." Rex eyed his best friend almost venomously. "Forget it."

"What?" Zeke asked. "I don't mind. And Rae shouldn't have to pay for everything."

"The answer is still no," Rex pressed.

"Why?" Zeke asked. "You'll take her money but not mine?"

"She's family," Rex argued. "It's different."

Zeke didn't react overtly, but I could tell something inside him broke a little. "I always thought we were family."

"We are," Rex said. "I didn't mean it like that..."

"Then let me help you," Zeke said. "I wouldn't offer if I didn't want to."

Zeke was always a good friend to Rex, and I appreciated that even if I never showed it. I wouldn't know what to do with myself if Jessie and Kayden weren't by my side every day. "I think it's a good idea," I said. "That way neither one of us takes a huge hit."

"I don't know…" Rex sighed anxiously. "I'm not even sure if I'll be able to pay you back."

"You will." The bowling alley was a dump. It was old, and the walls were gray. If we spiced it up, it would attract families as well as the younger crowd. There were tons of bars and shops around it, and it was the only bowling alley within twenty miles. It had all the potential.

"And even if I can, it'll take me a while," Rex said. "I won't be able to reimburse you overnight."

Zeke gave him an irritated look. "We both went to graduate school. How stupid do you think we are?"

"Well, I think Rae is one of the dumbest people I've ever met. You, on the other hand, are pretty damn gifted." Rex downed the rest of his beer then returned the empty glass to the coaster.

Ryker eyed us back and forth until he spoke. "Is this how all your conversations go?"

"What do you mean?" Rex asked.

"You're vicious to each other but have each other's backs at the same time?" Ryker moved his eyes to mine, and there was a hidden depth there I couldn't see.

Rex shrugged. "She's my sister and I hate her and everything, but...I kind of like her...sometimes."

He put out some good vibes so I reciprocated. "I kind of like him too...once in a blue moon."

***

"Nothing hits the spot quite like wings and beer." Ryker patted his flat stomach.

"Amen to that."

He put his hands in his pockets as he walked beside me, with Rex, Zeke, and Tobias up ahead. "I don't remember you from when I was in high school. It's strange because Rex and I used to hang out all the time."

"Well, he's five years older than me, so we weren't in high school at the same time. That's probably why."

He nodded in agreement. "It's funny that we've crossed paths again..."

"Yeah. And my dog didn't need to hunt you down for it to happen."

He chuckled. "Maybe you're the one who can sense where I am, not Safari."

"That's creepy..."

"A bit stalker-ish, huh?" he said with a laugh.

"Yeah. I like hot guys as much as the next woman, but not enough to creep around."

"Hot guy?" He looked at me with a smile on his face and a smolder in his eyes.

"Duh. Like you've never looked in a mirror."

He faced forward again, that smile still there. There was a slight tint to his cheeks, or perhaps I was just imagining that. "Want to come over?"

Last time he asked me out, he said the same thing. There was no invitation to dinner or the movies. "Straight for the kill, huh?"

He didn't seem apologetic about it. "We can do the whole date thing, but the only thing we're going to be thinking about over dinner is hitting the sheets. We're attracted to each other, so why don't we just skip ahead? Get to the good stuff?"

"Isn't the good stuff even better when there's a buildup? When you get to know each other?"

"Or we can get to know each other in an intimate way..." He said exactly what he wanted without any shame. No other guy could pull that off without looking like an asshole. Ryker was deadly handsome and carried himself with a lethal dose of confidence. He got what he wanted with little effort, and he probably had to do far less most of the time.

He came closer to me, his arm brushing past my shoulder. "What do you say, sweetheart?"

Even his voice aroused me. He could say anything and get my blood pumping. The immediate attraction held the kind of heat that could start a wildfire in the middle of a field. I turned down his offer once and went on a date that still left a bad taste in my mouth. I didn't want to do that again.

I wasn't ignorant. Ryker threw signals all over the place that told me he was a bit of a player. He made panties melt with just a smile, and he had a sign across his chest that said heartbreaker.

But I wanted something good after the dry spell I'd been through. I wanted heat and passion without the complications. While I wanted to find Mr. Right and my happily ever after, I wanted to be satisfied as I waited for him to come into my life. "Okay."

Now he grinned from ear-to-ear. "I was hoping you would say that."

"But I have to go home first. Then I'll meet you there."

"Why don't we just go now?"

"Because my brother will be a little bitch about it if he knows."

Ryker eyed Rex up ahead then turned back to me. "Why would he care?"

I rolled my eyes. "He's weird when it comes to boys. When he didn't live with me, it was much easier for me to date. But if I bring a guy back to my apartment or don't come home until the following morning, he flips out."

"Does he bring women back to the apartment?"

"All. The. Time." I couldn't count the number of times a girl in just a thong appeared in the kitchen when I was making breakfast before work. "It's a double standard thing. He's just protective of me, not that I need it."

"You don't strike me as the kind of woman to put up with it."

"I'm not," I said firmly. "I've told him off before, but it hasn't changed anything. Since the arrangement is temporary, it's just easier to tiptoe around him. And since you're his friend, it would be a million, zillion times worse. I would never hear the end of it."

"I can understand that last part."

"So, how about I meet you in an hour?"

"I guess I can wait for a little while." He gave me a smolder as he brushed up against me.

"You won't get started without me, will you?"

"I might...but I'll be thinking about you."

***

Rex and Zeke were in the living room when I grabbed my purse and prepared to leave. I shaved every inch of my body except my arms, eyebrows, and head, and I changed into a sexy pair of black panties. "I'm going out with Jessie. See you later."

Rex didn't turn around, but he raised his hand in goodbye. "See ya. Wouldn't wanna be ya."

I couldn't keep the sarcasm back. "Good one..."

Zeke turned around and actually gave me his attention. "What are you guys up to?"

"Not sure yet," I said. "But it probably has something to do with alcohol."

"You want more after today?" Zeke asked in surprise.

"You know me," I said. "I'm like a well."

"Well, have fun. Call me if you need a ride."

"If I'm calling anyone, it's Rex. That asshole owes me big-time."

Rex still didn't turn around. "I thought you were leaving."

"Go to hell."

Rex gave me the bird while his eyes were still glued to the screen.

***

Ryker had a nice apartment close to the water. It was on the top floor of the building, and the elevator took me right to it.

Was he loaded?

When the elevator reached his floor, the intercom started to ring like a phone. Ryker picked up after a few rings. "Ryker."

I stood there awkwardly, unsure what device to speak into. "It's Rae..."

"I was wondering when you would get here." The door opened and revealed his living room. The windows reached from the floor to the ceiling, and dark mahogany wood made up his floorboards. The walls were gray with white trimming, and his furniture was the color of cream.

I walked into the apartment and heard the doors close behind me. I took a look around and tried not to gawk at all the expensive things he owned. Working as a researcher for COLLECT gave me a great salary, but it was nothing compared to this. In just his living room alone, everything was more expensive than everything I owned put together.

Ryker emerged from the left, wearing sweatpants that fit low on his hips. Even when he was dressed casually, he looked sexy. His hair was a little messy like he didn't comb it after he got out of the shower. But he probably knew I was going to run my fingers through it and mess it up anyway. "I'm glad you're here." He walked right up to me and slid my purse down my shoulder. Then he set it on the table beside us in a fluid motion.

Now that we were alone together, the heat started to kick in. My body warmed up like a motor that hadn't run in a long time. It took me a while to reach full capacity, but when I was there, I was ready.

Ryker stared into my eyes with all the confidence in the world. Now that there were no witnesses, he stared at me like prey. His eyes moved across my body, like he was picturing exactly what he would do when he reached each spot.

His fingers moved under my chin, and he had a slight hold on my face. I didn't usually like being held like that, in a possessive way, but I liked it when he did it. He gently maneuvered my face, forcing my lips upward toward his. He leaned closer to me, about to lean in for the kiss.

When his lips were just inches from mine, I closed my eyes. I was prepared to feel that all-consuming touch, that fire that burned me from head to toe. My body ached for his in a carnal way. Like an animal, I wanted to go at it with everything I had.

"I promise this kiss will be much better than the last one you had."

My lips lifted involuntarily, and I opened my eyes to stare into his.

His eyes remained serious, his attention focused purely on my mouth. He moved his fingers from my jaw to my neck. They wrapped around the area, getting a good hold on me. Then he gripped a fistful of hair, using it as an anchor to keep my lips pointed to his.

Then he slowly moved in and pressed his lips against mine. When they brushed against my mouth, they were soft. The touch wasn't aggressive the way his hand indicated. The kiss was slow, practically immobile. He just rested his mouth there, savoring the gentleness of the touch. Then he moved his lips with mine, kissing me purposefully. Breaths entered my mouth and my lungs. The heat from his fingers burned my skin, constantly reminding me I was his for the evening.

His free hand wrapped around my waist and hooked on to the opposite hip. He pulled me against his chest, the curve of my breasts pressing right against him. I'd been a tomboy my whole life, but Ryker definitely made me feel like a woman.

He deepened the kiss but didn't increase the pace. The kissing was just as slow as it was in the beginning, but I loved it that way. There was no rush to reach the finish line. The journey itself was just as fulfilling.

Ryker pulled away slightly and looked down at my face. My lips were lonely the second his were gone. My heart kicked into overdrive at the slight halt. Ryker brushed his lips past mine in a teasing way before he kissed the corner of my mouth. Then he started to kiss me again.

My arms circled his neck, and with a mind of their own, my fingers snaked into his hair. It was soft like I suspected it to be, and the curls at the ends were slightly coarse.

I loved feeling the details of his features under my fingertips. His smell flooded my senses, and the scent was forever ingrained in my mind.

Effortlessly, Ryker scooped me up by my ass then lifted me into him. My legs automatically hooked around his waist like my body anticipated the movement. His lips moved to my neck, and he kissed the hollow of my throat in a seductive way.

He carried me past the window and into the hallway. All the doors were closed so I didn't know where they led, but his lips were distracting me too much to truly care.

We entered his bedroom and he gently laid me on the bed, rolling with me on top of the comforter. His thighs were between mine, and his hand returned to my hair as he kissed me on the mouth.

I ran my hands down his chest and felt the definition of his physique through his t-shirt. When I reached his waist, I moved my hands underneath the fabric and felt the bare skin. His stomach was all grooves and abs, and his chest was rock-hard. An indecipherable moan escaped my lips as my body entered a new realm of arousal. I was ready for him the second I walked into his apartment. I couldn't remember the last time I had sex, and I was excited that this would have a happy ending. Ryker didn't strike me as the kind of guy to leave a girl hanging.

One hand moved to my jeans, and he unbuttoned the top with ease. He kissed me at the same time, not breaking his concentration while he did two things at once. Once the zipper was done, he leaned back on the balls of his feet and pulled the pants down my legs. When I was just in my underwear, he looked at the black panties I wore. His eyes honed in on the area like it was a target. Then he widened my legs with his hands and pressed a kiss in the center of the fabric.

My hands immediately curled over his, and I moaned at the touch. The heat of his mouth felt so good against the sensitive area. I wanted him to keep going but would never be so desperate to ask for it.

He moved up my body again then pulled my top off. Just like with the jeans, he unbuttoned the clasp with a single hand. Once it fell loose, he kissed the valley between my breasts then sucked each of my nipples. He gripped one tit and squeezed it aggressively.

All this foreplay was making me writhe. I was already soaked and ready to go, but that didn't mean I wanted it to end. Listening to the sound our mouths made when we kissed, and noting the sound of our heavy breathing was a turn-on in itself.

I grabbed the bottom of his shirt and quickly yanked it over his head. The slab of concrete that made up his chest and torso was exactly what I hoped it would be. His skin was tan like he jogged shirtless, and the muscles of his arms and shoulders were even better.

I pulled his sweatpants down and took the boxers with them, wanting to get him naked as quickly as possible. When his cock popped out, I released a moan of joy.

Ryker gave me a heated look then moved two fingers to my entrance. He gently massaged the area before he slipped two fingers inside. My hands went to his biceps, and I looked at the desire written all over his face. He pulsed inside me before he slowly removed his fingers. "Big dick. Tiny pussy. Good sex." He kissed my stomach before he opened his nightstand and grabbed a foil packet.

I took it from his hands and did the honors. My fingers rolled the latex onto his length all the way to the base. Feeling his dick in my hands was hot as hell. I measured it with my fingers and realized it was nine inches. The fact that it was thick made it seem even bigger.

He positioned himself over me then kissed me slowly. The embrace was slower than it had been minutes ago. Now he seemed to be stalling, building up the moment when our bodies would combine.

I was anxious and needy. All his touches turned me on beyond capacity. Now I just wanted him deep inside me. I grabbed his hips and gave him a gentle pull.

He ended the kiss and pressed his forehead to mine. Then he did as I silently asked and pressed the tip of his head inside me. The thickness stretched me right from the beginning, making me feel full.

Ryker released a quiet moan as he slowly inserted his shaft inside me. My body needed a moment to acclimate to his large size. With every stretch of my body, there was slight pain. But there was so much more pleasure than anything else.

He slowly made the descent, entering one inch at a time. Once he was completely sheathed, he remained still and tensed above me, savoring every second.

I gripped his shoulders and dug my nails into his skin. I did it harder than I meant to and may have drawn blood, but the hormones inside me were responsible for it. My head rolled back automatically, and I arched my back. Nothing could describe how good the sex was.

And we'd barely started.

He slowly rocked into me, his length sliding past all the fluid my body produced for him. Sometimes he stared at my tits, and other times, he looked at my face. The look in his eyes told me he was enjoying it as much as I was.

My fingers moved into his hair and felt the strands. I twisted them, feeling the sweat that started to accumulate on the back of his neck. He thrust into me harder with every minute, making the headboard tap against the wall.

The night had only just begun, yet I felt that distant sensation form deep in my gut. It was a hot, fiery star that fell from the heavens and burned as it traveled across the sky. Every fiber of my being had come alive from the long sleep I had. It was the strongest climax I'd ever had, and I knew that before it even hit.

I bit my bottom lip and gripped his biceps as the unstoppable pleasure hit me like a bulldozer. It crashed into me hard and shattered me to pieces. My mouth formed an O, and I started to moan. I panted and yelled, loving the way I automatically constricted around his dick. I came all around him, providing more lubrication than he would ever need.

When the moment passed, I was suddenly covered in sweat and heat. But it still felt good, so I didn't want it to end. My hands moved down his back, and I felt the clear definition there. Every muscle was defined and toned. I could sketch the anatomy of the human body just by touching him.

"Mmm..." He put more weight on his arms as he leaned farther over me, giving me longer thrusts as he moved.

I wanted the reins for a little bit. After that performance, he deserved to lie back and let me do some of the work. I gripped his shoulders and rolled him to his back, clinging to him as I moved. His dick slipped out then landed with a noticeable thud against his stomach.

I balanced with the balls of my feet on either side of his hips and pointed his tip at my entrance.

Ryker stared at me with lust and awe. His hands moved underneath my ass cheeks, and he guided me down his length, wanting me to take him all in. Then he gripped my hips as he lay back on the pillows.

I gripped his waist and bounced on his dick, using my glutes and thighs to keep up the pace. Even when I felt the burn, I kept going because it felt so good.

Ryker loved it. "Fuck, baby." He thrust into me from underneath, wanting even more.

My hands moved to this chest, and I bounced up and down, taking in his big dick over and over. I didn't think I could have another orgasm, at least that quickly, but I felt it start all over again. That was rare for me and could only happen if I was particularly horny.

Or because the guy was particularly good in bed.

A moan came from the back of his throat. "Sweetheart, I can't last that long if you keep this up."
My nails dug into his skin and I moved harder, working up a sweat across my chest and shoulders. My hair stuck to the moisture and couldn't move. "I'm about to come again anyway."

"In that case…" He pressed his thumb against my clitoris then rubbed it aggressively. He moved in a circular motion, just the way I liked. The pressure was good, but he applied more the longer we moved together. When he gave it to me hard, I knew he was about to explode.

"Right there…"

"Come on, sweetheart." He closed his eyes and breathed hard, fighting off his urge.

I didn't tell him when I reached my threshold because my yells and screams were sufficient. I gripped him for balance then shoved him far inside me, enjoying the way he throbbed from within.

He gripped my hips and moaned with me, reaching his point at the exact same moment. He breathed through the pleasure and became red in the face.

I stayed on top of him as I wound down, suddenly aware of how sweaty and hot I was. We both worked our ass off during that rendezvous but all the effort was worth it.

I slowly pulled him out of me and felt the tenderness from his semi-hard dick. Then I lay beside him, still catching my breath.

He lay there in silence before his hand moved to mine and gripped it. He didn't cuddle with me because it was way too hot for either one of us.

After that workout, there was no way I could walk home. I was exhausted and satisfied. All I wanted to do was go to sleep and worry about it in the morning. I grabbed my phone from the nightstand and sent out a quick message to Rex.

Hammered. Staying with Jessie.

I sent a text to Jessie just in case Rex asked about it. *If Rex asks, I was with you tonight. I'll tell you the details later.* I tossed my phone on the nightstand and closed my eyes. Almost immediately, I was asleep.

***

"Morning, sweetheart." Ryker kissed my neck until I woke up.

It was a great way to start my day. "Morning."

He kissed my shoulder then my chest. "Sleep well?"

"Yeah. Your bed is comfy."

"You were able to sleep without Safari?" A teasing note was in his voice.

"Once in a while." I opened my eyes and looked up into his face. He was leaning over me, resting on his elbows.

"You look pretty in the morning."

"I do?" My makeup must be smeared all over my face. My mascara was probably running and my hair had to be a mess. Since I didn't look like Miranda Kerr, I couldn't just wake up and roll out of bed.

"Yeah." He kissed the corner of my mouth.

That lit me up all over again.

"Sorry to wake you. I just wasn't sure if you had work or something."

"You don't?"

"Not yet. I don't start my job for another week."

"That must be nice." I sat up and looked at the time. "Damn, I do need to get going. I was going to head home last night, but I was too tired."

"It's okay. Want to take a shower? I can make you some breakfast."

"No, I'm okay." I quickly dressed myself then walked to the mirror on top of his vanity. My hair was a bird's nest, but I managed to fix it with my fingers. My makeup wasn't running, but it was non-existent. I must have sweat it off the night before.

Ryker walked me to the door, wearing his sweatpants and a t-shirt. I was jealous he got to lounge around the house while I had to go to work and study pH levels and helpful bacteria. "Last night was fun."

"It was." Without saying anything, he made it clear what last night was. It was just a fling between two acquaintances. I probably should have just stayed away from him, but I really needed my fix. Actually, I didn't have any regrets. One-night stands could be an incredible experience depending on the way you looked at it. We would be able to keep it between us, and no one would ever know about it. It would be our dirty little secret. "I'll see you around." I leaned in and gave him one final slow kiss. "I wanted to take that to go."

He smiled, and it was the kind of smile that reached his eyes. "Do you need a box?"

"No. I'll keep it in my back pocket."

Ray of Light

Chapter Four

Rex

If Rex asks, I was with you tonight. I'll tell you the details later.

I stared at the text message with squinted eyes. Did it say what I think it said? I read it again and cocked my head to the side, unsure what to make of it.

"What?" Zeke sat beside me, a beer sitting on his thigh.

"Rae sent me a weird text."

"What does it say?"

I handed the phone over.

Zeke read it aloud. "If Rex asks, I was with you tonight. I'll tell you the details later." He kept staring at the screen and read it again silently. "Did she send you anything else?" He scrolled up and saw the previous message she sent. "Hammered. Staying with Jessie."

I took the phone back. "I think she meant to send that last one to Jessie but sent it to me by mistake."

"But why would she lie?"

That was my concern. Rae never lied to me. She told me the fat, ugly truth right to my face—every time. "I haven't got a clue."

Zeke stared off into the distance, his thoughts hidden behind his eyes. "Do you think she hooked up with someone?" The hollowness of his voice fell even on my ears.

"I don't know. If so, I hope it wasn't with Ryker."

Zeke immediately tensed in irritation. "He's the biggest player I've ever known."

"Bigger than both of us combined."

Zeke took a long drink of his beer, silently brooding. "She's too good for him."

"I know." I teased my sister a lot, but I truly thought the world of her. We both had a hard life growing up, and she still came out on top. She was never pompous with her success, and even though she was smarter than me, she never belittled me. When I hit a financial crisis, I didn't even have to ask if I could move in with her. She just offered.

"Are you going to talk to her?"

"I don't know what I'm going to do." She and I butted heads like opponents on the battlefield, but there were unspoken rules between us. We never lied to each other, and in a complicated way, that's what made our relationship unique. No matter how dark the sky became or how difficult times got, I could always rely on her. But if she couldn't be honest with me, then something was up.

"I can say something to her," Zeke offered. "Our relationship is a little different."

"No." It had to be me.

Zeke backed off, knowing this wasn't his territory. "Okay."

Ryker was a decent guy, but I'd seen him do a lot of things that would make any brother forbid him from being near his sister. I just assumed Ryker understood Rae was off limits. And if he touched her, I'd have something to say about it. Actually, my fist would.

Zeke set down his bottle on the coffee table and rubbed his temple like he had a migraine.

"You okay, man?"

"Yeah, I'm fine." He stared at the ground and appeared to be lost in his own world. "I should go." He left the couch and grabbed his keys before walking out. He didn't say goodbye or anything else.

Something was bothering him.

***

I just finished a pot of coffee when Rae walked inside. She wore the same clothes from the night before, and her hair was in a bun. She looked tired but rested at the same time.

"Hey." She tossed her purse on the counter along with her keys.

"Hey." I poured a mug of coffee.

"How was your night?"

She never made chitchat with me, and I suspected she was only doing it now out of guilt. She lied to me when she shouldn't have. In fact, she could have said nothing at all. If I were worried about her, I would have texted her. But she didn't need to report to me like I was her dad. "Good. Yours?"

"Good."

"What did you and Jessie do?" I kept the edge out of my voice so she wouldn't know how irritated I was.

"You know, we hit up a few bars and wreaked havoc all over the city."

"Sounds like fun..."

"Then I crashed on her couch."

"Your neck must be sore."

"Eh." She shrugged then massaged it. "Well, I need to get ready for work. When I'm off, we'll talk about all the adjustments for the bowling alley."

"Cool." I had to get to work too. Working behind the counter was boring as hell. I wish I could afford a worker to do it for me.

"Alright." She walked down the hall and went into the bathroom.

I stood at the counter and kept drinking my coffee.

***

"I'm taking off." I shut the register then washed my hands vigorously.

Helena stood at the counter, scrolling through Facebook on her phone. "Okay. See you tomorrow." She was covered in ink from head to toe, and her black hair had a few streaks of purple in it. She was pierced from her earlobes to the tops of her ears.

She was one hot piece of ass.

The second she turned eighteen, she came here and asked for a job. She needed to move out of her parents' place and get her own space. I said yes, of course.

"Call me if you need me."

She gave me a flirtatious look. "I always need you, Rex."

A shiver moved down my spine, and my dick hardened in my jeans. I wanted to take her in the back and fuck her on my desk. But she was ten years younger than me. Even though she was eighteen, she was still so young and ignorant. I had a feeling she was more delicate than she seemed.

I headed to the apartment and walked in to see Rae and Zeke sitting at the kitchen table. Chips and salsa were on the surface, as well as a few bottles of beer. Rae had her laptop out, and Zeke sat there with his phone on the table.

"The life of the party is here." I tossed my keys on the entryway table then opened a beer.

"Yay..." Rae's voice was full of sarcasm, like always.

"Helena is keeping an eye on the alley. And she looks damn fine doing it." I sat at the table beside Zeke.

"Be careful," Zeke warned. "Young girls can be clingy."

"That tattoo girl with all the piercings?" Rae asked. "Rex, you better stay away from her. She's way too young for you."

"Get off my back," I said. "If I were going to screw her, I would have done it by now."

"You shouldn't have hired her to begin with." Rae opened her laptop.

"What's wrong with her?" I asked. "Just because she's a little rough around the edges?"

"No," Rae said. "Because she's a terrible worker. How many complaints have you gotten because of her?"

A lot. "She's fine. I'm not going to fire her if that's where this is going."

"Obviously," Rae said. "But don't keep hiring chicks just because they're hot."

"They bring business," I argued.

Zeke shrugged. "True."

Rae rolled her eyes. "Sorry, do you want to run a bowling alley or a Hooters?"

My eyes widened, and I looked at Zeke.

He had the same look on his face. "Dude, that would have been sick."

"Goddammit! Why didn't I do that instead?" That would be my biggest regret.

Rae was used to the two of us so she ignored us. "Let's focus on what you do have."

"Let's sell it and open up a Hooters," I said. "Hot chicks with big tits. Perfect."

"I'll go in with you," Zeke said.

Rae didn't seem the least bit surprised. "Why don't you just open a strip club?"

Zeke nodded vigorously. "I like that idea."

"That really is perfect," I said. "Let's just sell the bowling alley—"

"We aren't selling the bowling alley," Rae said with unusual patience. "You wouldn't even get half of what you paid for it. Let's work on the place and get business up. Maybe when things are rolling, you'll have enough money to open a second business."

"That would be awesome." Girls would be dancing around me every day—and I'd be getting paid for it.

"So, let's focus." Rae was always the serious one of the two of us. I looked after her, but she had the personality of a drill sergeant sometimes. "We need to remodel the outside. A new coat of paint and a sign would do wonders. But we should wait until the rainy season passes. Otherwise, it'll just run right off."

"True," Zeke said.

"We can work on the inside now," Rae said. "Having a bar should draw people in. Maybe not a full bar, but at least something with beer and wine. If you have too many options, it might draw in shady people. Remember, this is a family place."

"Got it," I said.

"I think an arcade would help too. Keep the environment friendly."

"Aren't those gaming machines expensive?" I asked.

"We can get refurbished ones," Zeke said. "If we keep our eyes open on Craigslist, we should be able to get good stuff for a reasonable price."

"Cool," I said.

"We're going to have to tear out that carpet," Rae said. "It smells like ass."

"Hey, I have the janitor clean it," I argued.

"It still smells like two hundred cats came and peed all over it." She made the notes on her computer.

I turned to Zeke and gave him a look that said, "Really?"

He shrugged then nodded.

Damn.

"With all these changes, the place will look brand new," Rae said. "And I really think people will come flocking in."

"And then I can hire more staff so I don't have to be there all the time." Running a business had its positives, but also its drawbacks. Since I couldn't afford much help, I was working all the time. I just wanted to work in the morning then leave.

"I'm not sure when that's going to happen, Rex. Most business owners work their asses off for years before that happens." Zeke gave me a sad look.

"Ugh." I covered my face and sighed.

Rae started up her usual argument. "You could have invested in—"

"I bought the bowling alley. It's done." I held my hand up so she wouldn't keep yipping like a small dog.

Rae shut her mouth, but there was a bit of attitude in her eyes.

"So, how much is all of this going to cost?" Or did I not want to know?

"I won't be certain until I get an estimate," Rae said. "But after eyeballing it, I would say...at least forty thousand."

I almost fell over. "Forty thousand? Dollars? Please tell me you mean pesos."

Zeke nodded. "That sounds about right. The bar will be the most expensive part. And I think you should have food too. Pizza and fries or something."

I covered my face with my hands. "I'm going to be sick."

"Maybe you can have a consignment agreement with a business," Rae said. "Like Pizza Hut or Starbucks. They run their business inside the bowling alley, and you get a profit from their revenue since they're using your facility."

"But would they want to open a business in a bowling alley that has no customers?" Zeke asked.

Rae nodded. "Good point."

"Hold on," I said. "I'm still stuck on the forty thousand."

"Rae and I will split it," Zeke said. "That way it's not too much money for either one of us."

"Too much money?" My eyes almost fell out of my head. "How much money do you have just lying around?"

"It's called a savings account," Rae said.

"And I'm a doctor," Zeke said. "In case you forgot."

"But even then," I said. "I can't take that kind of money from you guys—not when I'm not sure if I can ever pay it back."

"We understand the risk, Rex," Rae said.

"I can't let you guys do it." I shook my head. "I'm sorry."

"Then you're going to go under in a year," Rae said. "Two tops."

"She's right," Zeke said. "I would much rather invest into this than see you lose it right off the bat. In that instance, you would be losing way more money than we would be investing."

"And I really think it could work," Rae said. "It's all about the environment. If people don't feel comfortable, they won't come. Why do you think everyone loves Disneyland? It's because it makes people feel good. You need to do something like that."

"Well, I've never been to Disneyland, so I don't know what you mean." I was pretty sure Rae hadn't either.

"It's just the idea," Zeke said. "If your place is a dump, you aren't going to attract anyone. No one is going to hang out there on a Saturday if it's rundown and old."

"I guess I know what you mean," I admitted.

"So, we need to make this place a hot spot," Rae said. "A place where everyone wants to hang out."

"Even if this plan works and I have more customers than I can serve...who knows how long it'll take me to pay you back. It may take me years. Ten years." Did they really understand that?

"We know," Zeke said. "And we're both cool with it."

"We aren't investing all of our money into it," Rae said. "We both have our own cash."

"Whoa." I gave Rae a hard look. "How much money do you have, kid?"

"I'm not telling you," she snapped.

"What are you saving for?"

"Uh, a house?" she said sarcastically. "A place with a yard so Safari can run around. My kids' tuitions."

"What kids?" I blurted.

"My future kids." Rae rolled her eyes. "You're more dense than I thought."

"Anyway," Zeke said. "You aren't running us dry. That's what she's trying to say."

I still felt bad taking anything from them. My sister had already let me live with her for months, rent-free. When things got really bad, Zeke paid for all my lunches and dinners. They did a lot for me when I didn't even ask. Could I take even more from them?

"Why don't we make it a theme?" Zeke said. "Like Groovy Bowl. We'll decorate the inside with tie-dye colors, and the wood strips for the alleys will each be a different color. Peace signs will be everywhere, and the chairs will be covered in fringe. We can even sell flower crowns to people who are really into it."

"That's not a bad idea," Rae said.

"Yeah, it's really cool," I said. "I'd bowl at a place like that, and I don't even bowl."

"We could have music from the 60s and the 70s overhead, and we can even have cardboard cutouts of The Beatles and The Doors so people can stick their faces through the holes and take a picture," Zeke said. "There are a lot of things we can do with it."

"Yeah," Rae said. "This is great." She made the notes on her computer. "Groovy Bowl. I like it."

"Maybe all the workers can be dressed as hippies," I said. "The girls will be wearing belly shirts and short-shorts." I smiled at the thought. "Ooh...their hair can be in a braid over one shoulder."

"Yeah." Zeke's face showed the same excitement. "They can dance on the counters every hour and—"

"Calm down, boys." Rae snapped her fingers. "You took it too far."

I sighed in defeat. "It's fun to dream about..."

"If we had a bowling alley that was also a strip club, you'd have serious problems," Rae said.

"My dick doesn't agree," I said.

Rae made a disgusted face. "Keep it PG around me. I'm your sister."

"Well, maybe you shouldn't—" I was about to call her out for sneaking out last night then lying to me about it. She must have hooked up with someone, probably Ryker, and that definitely wasn't

PG. But I didn't say anything because I wasn't sure if I wanted to confront her just yet. "Never mind."

Zeke looked at me like he knew exactly what I was going to say.

"That's what I thought." Rae had a confident look on her face like she just defeated me.

I let her keep thinking that—for now.

***

I went to the library then headed to the counter near the back of the building. Kayden was there. Her blonde hair was pulled back in a high ponytail, and the strands were in large curls. Her soft hair had a particular shine to it, like it was made of honey and silk. She wore black-framed glasses on her face.

I'd never seen her wear glasses before.

When I reached the counter, her eyes were glued to her computer. She was typing with concentration. Without looking at me, she said, "I'll be with you in just a second."

"Okay." I wasn't in a hurry.

When she recognized my voice, she looked up. Surprise flashed across her face, and she must have realized she was wearing her glasses because she hastily yanked them off and tried to set them on the counter. But instead, she dropped them on the ground. She bent down to pick them up, and when she came back up, she smacked her head on the counter. "Ouch..."

I leaned over the counter and looked down at her. "Kay, are you okay?"

"I'm fine." She rubbed the back of her head then stood up. When her face was revealed, it was red. She didn't look angry or appear to be in pain. It seemed like she was embarrassed more than anything else. "Uh, hi." She fixed her hair, looking flustered.

"Is your head okay? Want me to take a look?"

"No. I'm fine." She waved me off, her voice high-pitched.

I looked at her glasses on the counter. "I didn't know you wore glasses."

"Oh." She eyed them then tossed them in a drawer. "I only wear them once in a while. It's not like I need them or anything."

"I thought they looked cute on you."

The redness left her cheeks and she became pale. She stared at me with wide, unblinking eyes. She didn't even breathe.

Kayden was always quiet and shy. It surprised me that she and my sister were such good friends. Rae was wild, obnoxious, and wouldn't shut the hell up. Kayden couldn't be more different. "I didn't mean that in an offensive way..." I just said she looked cute. It wasn't like I commented on her tits or something.

"I'm not offended," she said quickly. "I just..." Her voice trailed away and she broke eye contact, looking flustered all over again. "What brings you here?" She swallowed hard.

"I came here for a book."

"Oh. What kind?"

"A marketing book," I said. "Rae, Zeke, and I are going to remodel the bowling alley. I just wanted to brush up on a few things." Actually, I wanted to learn a few things. I didn't know much about anything.

"I can help you with that." She walked around the corner then joined me on the other side. She wore a tight, black pencil skirt with a pink blouse. She had a small frame and noticeable curves. I'd always thought she had a nice body. Her calves were particularly nice. They were always pronounced when she wore heels.

I followed her down the aisles until we found the right section. Then she looked at the different books by my side. "There're a lot to choose from."

"Do you have any recommendations?"

"Sorry, I don't. I don't usually read about marketing."

"What do you read?"

"Sorry?"

Why was she so skittish all the time? "What do you read? You know, for fun."

"Oh..." She nodded in understanding. "I like fantasy novels."

"Like dragons and stuff?"

She nodded, looking embarrassed.

"That's really cool."

"You think so?" She started to fidget in place. "You don't think I'm a nerd?"

"Of course not." Why would I?

She nodded then stepped back. "Well, there's the selection. Let me know if you need anything else."

"Thanks, Kay."

"Anytime." She walked away. Actually, she practically ran.

I watched her with a raised eyebrow before I turned my attention to the books.

***

I stayed in the library and read because I knew I wouldn't get anything done at home. I would drink

90

a few beers and watch whatever was on ESPN. At least staying here limited the distractions.

When I was finished, I returned the book to where I found it and headed back to the front. Kayden was still there, her glasses back on her nose. They were black with square frames. They made her face look stern, but somehow it worked for her.

When she saw me approach, the relaxed posture she had disappeared. She shifted her weight and became tense, like I was an enemy rather than a friend.

I'd known Kayden for a long time, so I wasn't sure what the problem was. "Hey. Almost off?"

"Yeah. The library closes right now."

"Cool," I said. "Want to get some food?"

"Uh..." She acted like I just invited her on a trip to Iran. "Sure."

"Kay, is there something wrong?"

"No. Why would anything be wrong?" She pulled her glasses off and stuffed them into a drawer.

"You're just...tense?" I couldn't explain it right.

"Oh. I've just had a long day. Don't mind me."

I took her word for it. "What are you in the mood for? That pizza place is just across the street."

"That works for me."

We left the library then entered the parlor. A few people were inside sharing a family-size pizza. I figured Kayden and I would just split something since they didn't sell anything by the slice. "Combination?"

"Sure."

I ordered the pizza and grabbed the drinks. After we filled the glasses at the drink counter, we took a seat at a table.

Now that I was alone with Kayden, I realized we didn't do a lot of stuff together, just the two of us. I saw Jessie all the time, and that was never awkward. But with Kayden, it seemed like something was off. Whenever we were in a group together, I didn't notice anything, probably because she and I never spoke one-on-one. "So...you like the library?"

"I do. I love it, actually." She had a soft voice, like a schoolteacher.

"What do you love about it?" I wasn't undermining her. I was genuinely curious.

She shrugged. "I grew up with books. It's nice to be surrounded by them all day."

"Do you like to read?"

"I read all the time. I probably read one a week, depending on how big it is."

My jaw dropped. "One a week? Shit, I can't read a book in a year."

She chuckled. "You read one today."

"But that was a fluke," I said as I waved my hand. "I'll probably never read again in my lifetime."

"Why is that?"

"Boring."

"Maybe you just haven't found a good book."

"Eh." I shrugged. "It's hard for me to sit still for long periods of time, unless I'm watching TV."

"TV is kind of like reading. You're immersed in a story, just on a more intimate level."

"When I say I watch TV, I mean I watch sports. So, if there's a book about sports, then there's some hope. But I doubt it."

She chuckled. "Not really."

"Then it's never gonna happen."

A few strands of hair from her ponytail fell over one shoulder, and she fingered them with her forefinger.

"What are you doing this weekend?"

"Not sure," she said. "Probably something with Jessie and Rae."

Unless Rae had other plans with her secret hookup. "I got tickets to see the Wombats. Won them on the radio, actually. You want to come?"

She stopped touching her hair immediately and froze on the spot. "You're asking me to go to a concert with you?"

Why was that weird? We did group stuff together all the time. "Yeah, I got six tickets. I figured I would invite everyone. I have one extra, so maybe I'll find a hot date or something."

"Oh…" The lights turned off in her eyes, and her hand slowly moved to her lap. She broke eye contact and stared at her thighs. "Yeah…that sounds like fun."

I eyed the kitchen and wondered if our pizza was ready. "Dude, I'm starving."

"Yeah, me too," she said weakly.

I pulled out my phone and scrolled through Facebook quickly before I looked at her again. "Seeing anyone?"

"Uh, no."

Now that I thought about it, I'd never seen Kayden with a guy before. Whenever we hung out, she never brought a date along. It surprised me since she was obviously beautiful. "Date much?"

"Occasionally…" She didn't ask me the same question in return.

The pizza finally arrived, and I was relieved we had something to do besides stare at each other and talk...or whatever it was we were trying to do. She put one slice on her plate and ate that at a snail's pace. I ate like a normal person and devoured half of it by myself.

"How's the bowling alley?" she asked.

"Pretty terrible. I don't know what I was thinking when I bought the place."

"You were investing your money," she said. "I think that's smart. Anyone else would have blown that money on something they didn't need, like a car or a vacation."

Finally, someone stuck up for me. "Thanks. I just wish I picked something better."

"You didn't know," she said gently. "So, it doesn't look like it's going to make it?"

"Rae and Zeke came up with a few ideas to attract more customers. They seem confident that it'll work."

"Rae is pretty smart, so I would listen to her."

"She's not that smart." My sister might be good at science, but she was dumb in every other way. Sometimes, she turned on the blender without a lid, and other times, she left the refrigerator door open all night. She lacked common sense, and if you ask me, that's the most important intelligence to have.

"You just say that because she's your sister."

"And you just say that because she's your best friend."

Kayden shrugged in defeat. "I guess you're right."

"I'm always right."

Kayden rolled her eyes.

I smiled because she finally loosened up a little. "You like the pizza?"

"It's delicious."

"You must come here all the time since it's so close to where you work."

"I usually bring a lunch," she said. "I love to eat out, but it doesn't taste as good when you're doing it all the time."

I didn't know what she was talking about. I ate out all the time and never got sick of it. Nothing could beat the convenience of it. Sometimes Rae cooked dinner and I devoured that, but usually she just wasn't in the mood.

"You're surviving living with Rae?" she asked.

"It's not that bad," I said. "She yells at me for a lot of things...but in her defense, she's right."

Kayden smiled. "I'm telling her you said that."

"You better not." I threatened her with just a look. "This stays between us. We're friends, right?"

Her smile slowly faded, and the glow in her eyes dimmed. "Yeah, we're friends."

"Well, friends keep secrets sometimes. So, don't tell her I said that. Damn, I'd never hear the end of it."

"I'll keep your secret," she said quietly.

"Besides, if she knows I know she's right, then she'll yell at me even worse when I piss her off."

"What exactly do you do?"

"Well, I make a mess in the kitchen and I don't clean it up. But think about it, after you cook something, don't you want to eat it? You don't want to let it get cold and gross while you do dishes."

"Why don't you wash the dishes after you're done eating?"

"Because I'm full and tired..."

"Not a good excuse, but I get what you're saying."

"And I leave my dirty laundry in the laundry room, usually on the floor. She doesn't like that very much. And I throw my dirty towels on the floor after a shower. She gets pissed over that too."

"Rae is pretty organized, so I understand her frustration." Sometimes Kayden talked like a robot, like she was constantly afraid she might say the wrong thing to me. She was thinking about her words before she said them—walking on eggshells.

I blurted everything out without thinking twice about it. If someone didn't like me, they didn't have to talk to me. "But I don't want to change, so I'll keep doing it until I move out."

Kayden chuckled. "Rae will love that."

"I'm lucky she puts up with me. She threatens to throw me out almost every single day, but I know she's bluffing."

"I don't know... If you push her hard enough, she might do it."

"Nah. I know my sister hates me, but she loves me too."

Kayden smiled. "She does."

"Besides, when I'm there, I can take Safari out to do his business. So...I'm doing her a huge favor."

"Yes, what would she do without you?"

I finished the last slice then wiped the grease from my fingertips with a napkin. "So, you're down for the show?"

She nodded. "I'll be there. Thanks for the ticket."

"No problem," I said. "It wouldn't be the same without you."

She stared at me without blinking. Slowly, a smile crept onto her lips.

"Well, I'll see you later. I've got to get home and...get yelled at by my sister."

Kayden laughed louder that time. "Have fun."

"Want me to walk you home?" I asked. "I don't mind."

She looked like she might take the offer, but then her face quickly changed. "It's okay. I usually take a cab because I don't like walking in heels after standing in them all day."

I nodded. "Good thinking. I'll see you later."

"Bye, Rex."

I fist-pounded her, but since she didn't know what I was doing, she awkwardly tried to hug me. "Don't worry. You'll get it next time."

Ray of Light

Chapter Five

Rae

I walked into the hair salon and spotted Jessie at her station. "Pack up your shit and let's go. Happy hour ends in an hour."

"Chill." Jessie wrapped up the hair dryer then returned it to the station. Then she quickly swept the hair off the floor before tossing her apron over the back of the chair. "Alright. Let's head out."

We left the salon then walked down the block to our favorite cocktail bar.

"How was work?" I was surprised Jessie didn't immediately ask me to spill the beans about Ryker. Knowing her, that would be the only thing she cared about.

"It was alright. I had this new client come in and she asked me to cut her hair and style it. But when I was done, she got pissed off and said it didn't look good on her. Like, how is that my fault? She's the one who picked it."

"Did she ask for her money back?"

"Yeah."

"Did you give it to her?"

"Hell no. That's not how I run my business."

"I wouldn't have given it to her either."

She put her hands in the pocket of her jacket. "And I don't care about losing a client. My schedule is so booked up that it really doesn't make a difference. Besides, I don't want to do her hair ever again. Fuck. That. Shit."

I chuckled and crossed my arms over my chest to fight the cold. "You did the right thing. She can go somewhere else and make them suffer."

"Poor soul…"

We entered the bar then got a table in the corner. We ordered our drinks, and once they were there, we downed them like shots.

"There we go." Jessie leaned back and sighed. "That's what I've been looking forward to all day."

"Me too." I wiped my lips with the back of my forearm.

"When's Kayden coming?"

I eyed my watch. "She should be here soon. She said she wanted to shower after work."

"Probably because she smells like dust from all those books."

"Yeah." I waved down the bartender and got us two more drinks. "Half-off drinks, so I'm ordering twice as many."

Jessie clanked her glass against mine. "Word."

Kayden entered the bar, her blonde hair giving her away.

"There she is." I waved her over.

Kayden smiled then came our way. She took a seat and eyed the empty glasses. "Wow. You guys didn't wait up."

"Like you wouldn't have done the same," Jessie said.

Kayden paused for a second before she finally nodded. "You're right."

"Yep." Jessie waved down the bartender so Kayden could order something.

Kayden got her glass and took a long drink.

Jessie eyed her. "Bad day?"

"It was just long." She didn't give any further explanation.

Jessie turned to me. "So, what's new with you?"

What kind of question is that? "What? I expected you to bite my head off with questions about the other night." I was surprised when I didn't even get a response the following morning after I left Ryker's.

"What happened the other night?" Jessie deadpanned.

"You're joking, right?" I asked.

Jessie pointed to her face. "Does it look like I'm joking?"

"You didn't get my text?" I know I sent it.

"Again, I have no idea what you're talking about," Jessie said.

"And I have no idea what's going on." Kayden occupied herself with her drink.

"The other night, I hooked up with Ryker. I didn't know what to tell my brother so—"

"Who's Ryker?" Kayden asked.

"Yeah?" Jessie said.

"I'll get to that in a second," I said quickly. "Anyway, I texted my brother and told him I was staying with you so he wouldn't get weird about it. Then I texted you and told you to be my alibi."

Jessie held up her hand, what she usually did when she was about to throw some attitude my way. "You're a grown woman who can do whatever she wants. Why are you lying to him? If you spent the night with some guy, you shouldn't have to hide it. And he's staying in your apartment. Remember that."

I rolled my eyes. "I know. But he always gets weird about it. Always."

"Tell him to grow the hell up," Jessie said. "He sleeps around, so what does it matter what you do?"

"He just cares about you," Kayden said. "You know, the protective brother."

I didn't care if he was brother-of-the-year. "I shouldn't have to lie. I admit that. But he's only living with me temporarily, so instead of going toe-to-toe with him, I'd rather just avoid the confrontation until he leaves."

Jessie eventually nodded in agreement. "I guess I see your point."

"It's just easier this way," I said. "And you know how Rex is. When he's pissed about something, he'll never let it go."

"I think he just wants to make sure you're being respected and treated right," Kayden said. "He doesn't wear his heart on his sleeve, but he clearly cares about you."

Jessie rolled her eyes. "Why do you keep defending him?"

"I'm not," Kayden said. "I'm just being the devil's advocate. It's always good to understand both points of view. Rex sees himself as a father figure for you. He clearly thinks it's his responsibility to look after you. It's sweet, actually."

"Sweet, my ass," I said. "He becomes a control freak."

Kayden shrugged.

"Maybe you should tell him off," Jessie said.

"I might," I said. "But I'll wait until he moves out so I don't have to see him every day."

"Good call," Jessie said.

"Back to my original point," I said. "I texted you to cover for me. I specifically told you not to tell Rex I wasn't with you that night. You don't remember that?"

"Girl, if I got your text, I would have known it." Jessie sipped her drink then ate the olive.

"But I know I sent it. Check your phone."

She sighed in irritation before she pulled it out of her bag. Then she opened up the screen where my text messages were listed. "Look. The last message I got from you was on Monday when you asked which brand of hair dryer you should get." She handed it to me.

That couldn't be right. I checked her phone and realized my message wasn't there.

"You probably didn't hit the send button or something," Kayden said. "I do that all the time."

I set Jessie's phone down before I pulled out my own. "I guess. You haven't talked to Rex then?"

"Nope," Jessie said.

"Phew." I pulled out my phone and looked at Jessie's conversation. It wasn't written in the text box, which was strange. I hadn't texted her anything else so the words should still be there even if I didn't send them.

"Maybe you texted someone else," Kayden said. "I do that all the time when I'm exhausted."

"I guess..." The only other person I texted was Rex, but there was no way I sent it to him. I opened his conversation then almost screamed. "No!"

"What?" Jessie and Kayden said together.

If Rex asks, I was with you tonight. I'll tell you the details later.

"God fucking dammit." I pounded my fist on the table. "I sent it to Rex instead."

Jessie's eyes widened. "You're serious?"

I threw the phone at her.

She checked the screen and saw the same thing I did. "Shit..."

I covered my face because I couldn't handle the horror. "No. No. No."

"She really sent it to him?" Kayden asked.

"Yep," Jessie said. "And it even says he read it."

"Kill. Me. Now." I slowly lowered my hands and wanted to rest my forehead against the table because I was depleted of all reason to live.

"That's awkward," Jessie said. "Has he said anything to you?"

"No." Which was weird, now that I thought about it.

"Hmm..." Jessie set down the phone and returned to her drink. "He obviously read it, so why hasn't he confronted you?"

"He's probably waiting to ambush me at the right time." Now there wasn't enough alcohol in the world to make me feel better. "And just yesterday, I went on and on about all the stuff we did together that night...and he knew I was lying the entire time."

"Ouch," Kayden said. "That's rough."

"See?" Jessie said. "You should have just told him the truth."

"Not now," I snapped.

"What are you going to do?" Kayden asked.

"I'm not sure," I said. "I guess I'll just wait for him to confront me."

"Or maybe he won't confront you at all," Jessie said. "If you felt the need to lie to him, then maybe he realized he's being too involved in your personal life. Maybe he took it as a sign to step back."

"Maybe...but I doubt it." I wish that were the case.

"What other explanation is there?" Jessie asked.

"I guess that's true," I admitted.

"Maybe he's let it go and moved on," Jessie said. "It has been a few days."

"True," I said in agreement.

"Now enough of that," Kayden said. "Who's Ryker?"

"Yeah," Jessie said. "He sounds hot."

"He is," I said. "Oh boy, he is."

"Spill it." Jessie snapped her fingers.

"Remember that guy I ran into at the park?" I said.

"Yeah," Kayden said.

Jessie nodded.

"Well, it's him. Apparently, he went to high school with Rex and Zeke so they're friends. He just moved back here from New York so they reconnected. We played basketball together, and afterward, he invited me over."

"Ooh..." Jessie rubbed her palms together. "And how was it?"

"Ah-maze-ing." Every second of it was a taste of heaven. "He had the right package and the right style. I left there feeling completely satisfied."

"I'm jealous," Jessie said. "Are you seeing him again?"

"I'm sure I'll see him around because he's friends with Rex, but we aren't going to go on a date or anything." We didn't even exchange phone numbers.

"That's it?" Kayden asked.

"He made it pretty clear he was just looking for a one-night stand. And I'm fine with that. I've been going through a dry spell, so it was nice to have something purely physical." Now that we were talking about Ryker, I was distracted from the ordeal with Rex.

"You don't think you'll sleep together again?" Jessie asked.

"Nah. The one time was fun, but I don't want to make it a regular thing. That gets too complicated." Feelings get involved, and it's too hard to walk away.

"So if he asked you out, you would say no?" Jessie asked incredulously.

"If he asked me on a date, I'd say yes in two seconds. But he'll never ask me. I'm not gonna hold my breath and wait for that to happen." Ryker was handsome and charismatic, but I knew a player when I saw one. Guys like that never changed, and when they did, it was only for someone really special.

And I knew I wouldn't be that special someone.

Kayden nodded. "You're right. Never wait around for a guy."

"Hell no," Jessie said. "At least you got your fix so you can move on."

"Yeah. And I definitely don't regret it. It was nice...really nice."

Both of them looked at me with envy in their eyes.

I needed to change the subject so they wouldn't keep staring at me like that. "What about you guys?" I asked. "What's new with you?"

***

Mr. Price came down to the lab near the end of the day. He wasn't very old, maybe in his late fifties, but he seemed frail. He walked slowly, like every step caused him pain. His smile wasn't as bright as it used to be. I wondered if I was the only one who noticed.

"How's it going down here?" Mr. Price approached my workbench and leaned on the counter.

"Pretty good. I have a few ideas I'm working on."

"You've always been a hard worker. I appreciate that." His hair had fallen out, and he was nearly bald. He used to be twenty pounds overweight, but now he was on the leaner side.

"I appreciate the opportunity to work here." COLLECT was nice because all the lab equipment was clean and new. The pay was great, and the benefits were awesome. If everything stayed the same, I intended to work there for a long time.

"You're a sweet kid." He patted me on the back. "I'm going to miss you."

"I'm going to miss you too, Mr. Price." He always infected the halls with his buoyant spirit. He was the kind of boss that made you feel appreciated. I never felt like a simple employee. I always felt like a person. "But I'm sure we'll still see each other."

"Yeah," he said quietly. "I'm sure we will."

"Is today your last day?"

He nodded. "It's weird to think I won't be walking down these halls anymore..."

"I'm sure it is." He opened this company and worked here for over thirty years. It was like a child to him. "What plans do you have for retirement?"

"You know, some traveling and whatnot."

"You think your son is ready to fill your large shoes?"

He chuckled. "He'll be fine. He's exceptionally bright. I'm not sure where he gets it from."

"You, I'm sure."

He clapped me on the shoulder and laughed. "You're too sweet. You're going to make a man very happy someday."

"I hope so."

"Don't accept anyone less than the best," he said. "You're too good for that."

I smiled. "Thank you."

"Well..." He stood up straight and looked tired. "I just wanted to come down here one more time."

I pulled him in for a hug and held it for a moment. "Thank you for everything, Mr. Price."

He hugged me tightly before he let go. "No, thank you." He gave me a smile before he headed to the entrance. He walked slowly, like he carried a heavy weight that I couldn't see.

***

I came home that evening and was immediately on alert. Rex hadn't confronted me about that text message, and I suspected he would eventually. Waiting around was the hardest part. It was going to lead to a fight, and I just wanted to get it over with.

I saw him in the living room. "Hey, how was your day?"

"Boring. Super boring." He didn't look over his shoulder to talk to me. A beer was sitting on the table, condensation beading against the glass. He hadn't been himself lately. He was usually talkative, and when he wasn't, he usually argued with me. But now he was docile and quiet.

I knew he was pissed. "Things will pick up, and then you'll be on your toes all day."

"Maybe."

"Well, I'm going to take a shower." I headed to the hallway.

"Are you actually going to shower?" he snapped. "Or is that your alibi?" His eyes were glued to the TV.

I froze on the spot, realizing the moment had finally come. I sighed quietly so he couldn't hear it before I walked into the living room. It was stupid to feel uneasy. It was my personal life, and he shouldn't stick his nose in it at all. But anytime my brother was upset, it put me on edge.

Rex refused to look at me. He didn't even glance my way.

I sat on the other couch, not wanting to be too close to him.

"What?" he said. "You aren't sure?"

I held my silence.

He finally looked at me when I remained unresponsive. There was anger in his eyes as well as disappointment. "Since you weren't with Jessie the other night, where were you really?"

I didn't bother acting innocent.

"Hmm?" he asked. "Or are you going to lie to me again?"

"Rex, where I was is none of your business, so I'm not going to answer."

He clenched his jaw.

"I'm sorry I lied to you. I just didn't know what else to say."

He rose to his feet quickly like he couldn't sit still. "I know you and I butt heads a lot. We're both argumentative and confrontational. But you're the one person in this world I can rely on. You're the one person who doesn't lie to me. But then you did. The best thing about our relationship is our brutal honesty. I don't hide anything from you, and I'm hurt you would lie to me like that."

Now he was making me feel guilty. "I shouldn't have lied. I know. But you need to stop sticking your nose in my personal life. I'm a grown woman with a big girl job. What I do is absolutely none of your business. You have no right to interrogate every guy I date and chase him off. It's completely unacceptable. If you didn't act that way, then I wouldn't have lied at all."

"Rae, I'm just looking after you. Every guy that comes through that door needs to know they can't mess with you. That's my job."

"No, it's not." I rose to my feet, feeling the anger kick in. "Rex, you aren't my dad. You don't need to act that way."

"Yes, I do. I'm all you have."

"I appreciate what you're doing, but I'm a big girl who can take care of herself. I don't need someone to look after me. Frankly, it's weird when you ask me about guys I'm seeing or push them around when you see them the following morning. It's really weird. I want you to stay out of it from now on. I don't ask about your personal life or get involved at all. You need to butt out of mine."

He crossed his arms over his chest, the same expression on his face.

"I only lied because I didn't want to explain where I was or what I was doing. It's awkward, and it makes me uncomfortable."

"Were you with Ryker?" The darkness in his eyes told me he would be pissed if my answer was yes.

"Rex, it's none of your business who I was with."

"He's not a good guy, Rae. He's my friend and everything, but he's not the kind of guy you should date. He's only after one thing, and when he gets it, that's it. He's gone."

"You think I didn't know that?" I asked incredulously. "I'm not oblivious to the world around me. I understand what's going on. Ultimately, it's my decision if I want to get involved with him, not yours."

"So, you were with him?" he pressed.

"That's not what I said."

"Well, were you?"

"Rex, it doesn't matter. Maybe I was with another guy. I don't tell you about my personal life, so you really have no idea who it could have been. Stop asking me stuff like that, and just drop it."

He sighed like that was the most difficult thing in the world.

"Rex, I love you. I'll always be here for you. You're the only family I have left, and I'll always cherish what we have. But I'm not going to budge on this. You need to back off. I mean it."

His anger started to dwindle with every passing second. He sighed again, like he knew what

I was saying was the truth. "It really hurt me when you lied to me. I don't want you to lie to me ever again."

"That's fair. I won't."

"Okay."

"And?" He better meet me halfway.

"You're right. What you do privately is none of my business. I know you aren't a kid anymore, so you don't need me to look after you. I get it. I do."

That was better than I hoped for.

"I meant well. I just want the best for you. Whoever you end up with needs to be the perfect guy in every way imaginable. I just... I took it too far. I'm constantly trying to protect you because I forget that you don't need me to protect you anymore."

"Thank you."

"It's just..." He rubbed the back of his neck. "I had to take care of you when I turned eighteen. I didn't know anything about raising a kid or being responsible for someone else. I could barely take care of myself. After I took you under my wing, I started to look at you in a different way...like you were my kid or something. I guess I'll always have that mindset, making sure you are happy and have everything you need."

It was hard to stay mad at him when he said things like that. "I know…"

"We really go at it sometimes, but I love you." He didn't look at me as he said it. "I'll try to be better from now on. I'll back off and just be your brother. It'll just…take me some getting used to."

That was all I asked for. "Thank you."

He put his hands in his pockets and stood there awkwardly. "So, no more lies?"

I shook my head. "No more lies."

He nodded and continued to stand there. "Should we hug or something?"

I smiled because the tension finally left. "I think we can hug…this one time." I crossed the living room and hugged him around the waist.

He returned my embrace and rested his chin on my head. "It's you and me against the world, Rae. And it'll always be you and me."

***

"The new guy started today." Jenny made notes in her lab book before she shut it forcefully.

"What new guy?"

"The new CEO." She rolled her eyes. "Let's see how he demolishes this place."

"You know, you're awfully prejudiced against someone you've never met."

She rolled her eyes again, dramatically. "His resume tells me all we need to know."

"Mr. Price is so sweet. I can't see him having a son that's any different."

"You just have a thing for old men."

"Do not," I argued.

"Whatever," she said. "You think he's the cutest thing in the world."

"Well, other than Safari, he is pretty cute. He said goodbye to me the other day, and it was so sad..."

"You'll be more sad when this guy puts you out of a job."

Since she was set in her ways, I didn't bother trying to change her opinion. Honestly, I doubted we would even know someone new was running the place. Jenny and I stayed in the lab all day, and we didn't cross paths with other workers in the company. We were pretty much quarantined.

"He might get rid of the research program altogether," Jenny said. "It's not like we make the company any money."

"That's not true. We're always finding ways to improve the system."

"But he may not think it's worthwhile."

I eyed the clock on the wall. "Jenny, why don't you take lunch?" Her negativity was starting to get on my nerves.

She put her hands on her hips as she considered it. "You know what? I could use a cigarette."

"Those things will kill you."

She shrugged as she grabbed her purse. "I'm probably going to die young anyway." She headed up the stairs and left the lab.

I kept working on my titrations when the office phone rang. I took the call and put it on speaker. "It's Rae."

"Hey, it's me." Jessie's bossy voice came through the phone. "Can you talk?"

"Yep. I've got you on speaker and there's no one else here."

"Great. So, what happened with Rex?"

"We got into a fight but we made up."

"That's it?" she asked. "It must have been juicier than that."

I paused to do a quick calculation then I kept going. "He was pretty upset that I lied to him. He says he doesn't want to have a relationship like that."

"Then you told him off?"

"Pretty much. Thankfully, he agreed to back off. Then he talked about how daunting it was to take care of me when Mom died. That got a little emotional…"

"Awe."

"We both apologized and agreed to move on. He even hugged me."

"Wow," she said. "That's the first one ever, right?"

I laughed. "I don't know about the first, but it's one of the rare few."

The door at the top of the stairs opened, and I heard it shut behind whoever came inside. It could have been Jenny because she forgot something or it could have been someone else entirely. "Jessie, I've got to go. I'll talk to you later."

"Bye, girl. Love you."

"Love you too." I hit the end button then ripped off my gloves so I could put on a clean pair. When I turned around to grab the box, I stopped in my tracks at the sight before my eyes.

Ryker stood there in a black designer suit. He wore a gray tie that brought out the brightness of his eyes. The usual scruff on his face was gone because he shaved that morning. He seemed just as surprised to see me as I was to see him. "Uh, hi…"

He stood with his hands in his pockets, taking me in.

"You're the new CEO?" How was that possible?

He finally came back to earth and stepped closer to me, retaining his coolness. "Yes. Unfortunately."

I felt self-conscious in my lab coat and half-assed bun. The only person who ever saw me down here was Jenny. And she usually looked like hell too. "I...I didn't realize that."

"Well, I didn't know you worked here either. I guess we're both surprised."

"Yeah." Why didn't Rex tell me that? He obviously knew. What was he thinking?

Ryker scratched his chin before he returned his hand to his pocket. "I've been going to all the departments to introduce myself. I know this change has been difficult on everybody. All I ever hear is how great my father is."

"He is," I said in agreement. "He's one of the sweetest, most generous men I've ever known."

Ryker stared at me without any reaction.

"But I'm sure you'll do great too."

"Hopefully." He came closer to my workbench then looked around the lab. "This is where you do all your research?"

"Yeah. It's a nice space. Your father gave us all the equipment and space we needed."

He nodded. "He always said the research department was the most important one."

He did? "That was sweet of him to say."

Ryker stared at the titration equipment hanging in front of me, seemingly perplexed by the way it worked. Then his green eyes turned back to me, deep like the moss on the north side of trees. "On to anything I should know about?"

"I am working on a project right now, but I'll tell you about it once I have promising data. There's no reason to get your hopes up."

"Are you the only one down here?"

"No. Jenny is here today, but she's at lunch. There are two other researchers too."

"I guess I'll have to stop by and see them another time."

"Yeah, that would be nice." It was the first time I'd seen him in a suit, and he looked damn good in it. Memories of our night together played in my mind. He was an exceptional kisser, the kind that melted your panties right off your legs. And the way he felt inside me was unforgettable. That night was just a one-time thing, but it was still fun to think about.

He must have been thinking about it too because there was a slight smile on his lips. "Rex invited me to see The Wombats with you guys this weekend."

"He did?"

"Yeah. Is it cool if I tag along?"

"Sure. I just have to warn you that I'm really loud, and I move around a lot."

A knowing look was in his eyes. "Yeah...I knew that."

My cheeks immediately flooded with heat.

He glanced over his shoulder at the door before he came closer to me. "Since we work together, and I'm friends with your brother, maybe we should talk about what happened. Is everything okay between us?"

"Of course." Why wouldn't it be?

He watched my face for a lie.

"It was a lot of fun, but when you try to do the same thing again, it's never as good as you remember it."

He tilted his head slightly.

"I would love it if we could be friends. I already like you, and I'm pretty sure you like me."

"I do like you."

"Then the past is in the past. It can be our little secret." I extended my hand to shake his.

He eyed it without taking it. "And that's it?"

"What do you mean?"

"You don't want to see me again? You don't expect anything?"

"If I did, this conversation would have gone much differently."

He finally took my hand. The warmth of his fingers felt good on mine. I could detect the dryness of his skin. I remembered the way his palms felt as they squeezed my tits.

I pulled my hand away and broke the contact. "So, is there anything you want to know about the company? Something your father didn't explain?"

"No. I think I'm good."

"Well, I'm always here if you have a question. I know I work in the lab, but I know a few things."

"I'm sure you do." He continued to stand there even though it seemed like the conversation was over.

The clock was ticking, and I had my specimens to run. In addition to that, I had to report everything in my lab report. It was a lot of tedious work because it was time-consuming. "Well, I should get back to work. I'll see you on Saturday."

He rapped his knuckles against the counter gently before he stepped back. "I look forward to it."

***

"Why didn't you tell me Ryker was taking over COLLECT?" It was the first thing I said when I walked in the door.

Rex stood at the counter with a meatball sandwich in his hands. He was about to take a bite before he was interrupted. "Huh?"

"Ryker is the new CEO of COLLECT. Why didn't you tell me?"

He eyed his sandwich, like he was sad he couldn't eat it because he had to talk. "I thought you knew."

"How would I know that?"

He shrugged. "You guys hang out. I assumed he told you."

I wanted to slap him upside the head sometimes. "You didn't even mention it in passing."

"Sorry. Geez." He finally took a bite of his sandwich, but the hot meatball and sauce melted through the bread and cheese and fell on the floor. He looked up at me, fire burning in his eyes. "I hate you."

I grabbed a paper towel and picked up the mess. "Finish eating then I'll yell at you." I tossed the paper towel and the meatball in the garbage.

"What are you doing?" he screamed. "Don't throw that away."

"It fell on the floor. Safari lies there. That's disgusting."

"It's still food." He fished it out then shoved it back into his sandwich.

I cringed and felt the vomit rise. "That's so gross."

He ate half of it in one bite. "Mmm...tastes delicious to me." He sat at the kitchen table and kept eating.

My brother was so disgusting. I didn't understand how he came home every weekend with a different girl. I mean, did they talk to him? Did they know how weird he was?

I sat across from him and waited until he was finished with his sandwich. "Can you talk now?"

"There're no more meatballs so the floor is open." He had sauce smeared across his face.

I waited for him to wipe it off.

He opened a bag of chips and started eating, oblivious to the shit on his face.

"Rex." I pointed to the corner of my mouth. "You have sauce everywhere."

"Eh. I'm still eating. I'll get it later."

Why did I bother?

"What were you saying?"

"Ryker said you invited him to the concert."

"Yeah. Is that cool?"

"I don't care." It didn't seem awkward between Ryker and me, so there shouldn't be any problem.

"So...are you seeing him?" He looked into his bag of chips and avoided eye contact with me. "I'm just asking out of curiosity so I know what to say when I'm around him."

"No, I'm not seeing him."

He didn't hide the relief on his face. "Okay."

"Ryker and I are just friends. We'll probably get closer since we work together. But that's about it."

"All the girls like him."

"Yeah, I'm not surprised." He had it all. He had money, looks, and smarts—the whole package. Not to mention, he was amazing in bed. And when he let his walls down, he was actually pretty funny.

"And he's a heartbreaker. That guy has never had a girlfriend since the day I met him. They just come and go."

"I figured." I understood it, but I couldn't help but feel bad for him. I didn't think there was anything wrong with one-night stands or casual sex but to avoid relationships altogether was downright lonely. Guys had come and gone in my life, but just because they didn't last forever didn't mean those relationships meant nothing to me.

"I'm glad you get the gist. He's no good for you."

I gave him the stink-eye.

"I mean...do whatever you want."

***

I wore dark jeans and a shiny black top to the show. I curled my hair and left it down so I could fling it everywhere as I rocked out. The Wombats were a new favorite of mine, and I was excited to shake my ass at the concert.

I opened the door to see Zeke on the other side. "Hey, are you excited?"

He looked me up and down. "You look hot."

"Oh." I glanced at myself automatically. "Thanks. You look tasty yourself."

He wore a short-sleeve gray t-shirt that showed off his nice arms. Zeke was like a brother to me, but I wasn't oblivious to the fact that he was good-looking. Anytime we went anywhere, girls cast their looks his way. And sometimes, they asked if I was his girlfriend before they put the moves on him. "Is the beauty queen ready to go?"

Rex shouted from his bedroom, "Shut the hell up, bitch."

Zeke chuckled. "I guess that's a no."

Safari came to the door wearing that same sad look on his face as every time I left the house.

"Sweetheart, I'll be home later." I gave him a good rubdown so he would feel loved.

He whined quietly.

"Don't worry. I'll be sleeping with you tonight." I kissed him on the nose.

He whined again.

Zeke watched our interaction. "It's like he understands you sometimes."

"He does." I stood up then shoved my cash and ID into my pocket. "Rex, hurry the hell up. I'm not going to be late."

"Shut up." Rex came down the hallway in jeans and a hoodie. "I'm coming. Geez."

"Let's head out." I gave Safari another pat on the head before I walked out with the guys.

"Got the tickets?" Zeke asked.

"Yeah," Rex said. "I've got them in my pocket."

We left the apartment then took a cab to the stadium. It was just a fifteen-minute drive, and when we got out, we saw the line.

"Jessie and Kayden are already here," I said.

"Sweet," Rex said. "We can cut in line."

"I knew those girls were good for something," Zeke said.

We located the other two then joined them in line.

"Oh my god." Jessie jumped up and down. "How excited are you?"

"Super duper." I clapped my hands excitedly.

"I'm going to get a Wombat hat," Kayden said. "I'm going to look so cute."

"Ooh...maybe I'll get one too." I'd look like a weirdo but whatever.

Rex eyed his phone before he answered it. "Yo, where are you?"

He must be talking to Ryker.

"We're toward the front of the line," Rex said. "Some of our friends got here early. Just keep moving up until you see me." He hung up and shoved the phone back into his pocket.

"Who else is coming?" Jessie asked.

"Ryker."

"Ooh...interesting." Jessie had a devilish look on her face. "So, does the girl code apply here? You slept with him so he's off limits."

"Not really," I said. "He's a player, so I don't think it matters."

"Really?" she asked.

"Yep," I said. "You can have him."

"Sweet," Jessie said. "Now this concert just got better."

Rex waved when he spotted him. "Yo, over here."

Ryker joined our group. He wore dark jeans that hung low on his hips with a black t-shirt. He looked good in anything he wore. And he looked particularly good naked. "Hey, thanks for letting me tag along."

Kayden and Jessie both stared at him like he was too good to be true.

Jessie pulled my ear to her lips. "Oh. My. God."

"I know," I said with a nod.

"And you're totally fine with me going for him?" Jessie asked. "Because I'm gonna."

I laughed. "He's all yours."

Jessie looked up to the heavens. "Thank God."

Ryker introduced himself to the girls. They shook his hand with weak grips, mesmerized by how pretty he was.

I was still attracted to Ryker, but my infatuation stopped after I got my kicks. I explored that avenue as far as it would go. Then I hit a dead-end. I wasn't the type of girl to keep ramming into a brick wall until it came down. I'd rather turn around and find a different route.

Ryker stood beside me. "Excited?"

"You know it."

"So, I guess that means we're coworkers."

I laughed. "No, you're my boss. I guess I can't get that hammered tonight."

"It's okay," he said. "I don't like stiff employees anyway. Besides, my dad is really fond of you. He'd be disappointed in me if I let you go."

"In that case, I'll probably be stealing a lot of paper clips and pens."

He laughed, showing his nice smile.

We moved to the front of the line and handed over our tickets. Then we filed into the stadium and found our seats on the floor. We were just ten rows back so we were close. I didn't need to worry about any heads getting in my way.

I was sitting between Zeke and Rex. On the other side of Rex was Ryker. Jessie sat beside him. She was making it a little obvious she was interested in him. Playing it cool was the best way to go, but Jessie had her own approach. She had the perfect hair and body, so she didn't need to worry about playing games. If she wanted something, she just took it.

I wasn't so blessed.

"I can't believe you slept with him," Kayden said. "He's soooo fine."

"I know." I'd probably picture that night when I had a session with my vibrator.

"And you're going to let Jessie scoop him up?"

"I really don't mind. He's not boyfriend material."

"The perfect ones never are…"

There was an opening band that played for nearly an hour. I occupied myself by eating nachos and drinking Coke. Zeke split it with me, and he kept eating all the good parts, where the chips were almost completely covered with melted cheese.

"Dude, get your own."

"Why?" he asked. "I can just be a freeloader. It's much easier."

"You're a doctor. I should be mooching off of you."

"I thought I wasn't a real doctor," he teased. "You can't play it both ways."

I shoved the rest of the nachos into my mouth and tried to get them down. "Now you can't eat them." I tried talking with my mouth full, but it was difficult.

"I hope you choke on that."

I managed to get everything down after a drink of my soda.

Zeke eyed his watch. "I hope it starts soon."

"Why? Is your bedtime soon?"

He gave me a glare before he tickled me. "What did you say, punk?"

I laughed then pushed him off. "Okay, okay. I'm sorry." I sat forward and crossed my legs.

"That's what I thought," Zeke said.

I felt eyes drill into me, and I could tell which direction they were coming from. When I turned to the left, I saw Ryker staring at me. He held the gaze without looking away. I was the one who turned first.

It was weird.

The band finally came out and the show began. They immediately played all their best singles, and that's when I started jumping around and singing at the same time. Kayden was into the music too. Zeke was fun no matter what we did, so he sang along with me.

Rex stood there, almost looking bored.

Ryker watched the band, looking cool and indifferent. Jessie kept clapping and tapping her hip against his. His hands were in his pockets, and every few seconds, his eyes moved to mine.

Eventually, I faced the other way so our eyes wouldn't cross paths anymore. I didn't want him to think I was looking at him. I really wasn't. I just kept feeling him looking at me.

Zeke grabbed my hand and started to spin me in place as we danced together. We were having so much fun that I forgot about Ryker's drifting looks and just had a good time. The beer, nachos, and soda were all kicking in at the same time.

And I got lost in the music.

***

I was dead tired after the concert. All I wanted to do was curl up with Safari and go to sleep. All the jumping around and singing wiped me out. There wasn't enough coffee in the world to keep me awake.

We stood in the endless line as we tried to file out of the stadium. It stretched on forever, so I knew we would be there for a while. Getting a cab would be nearly impossible.

"You holding up, champ?" Zeke asked.

I rubbed the corner of my eye. "Just tired." I yawned loudly, feeling my eyes moisten in response.

"Want me to carry you?"

A sarcastic laugh escaped my lips. "No, it's okay. I'm not a child."

"You weigh as much as a child."

"Maybe one that developed early."

We slowly moved to the front of the line. After thirty minutes of standing around, we finally reached the sidewalk.

"We're never going to get a cab now," Rex said. "We'll get there quicker if we walk."

Walk home? I'd rather sleep on the sidewalk.

"I drove," Ryker said. "I can take someone with me."

Jessie twirled her hair and batted her eyelashes.

"Well, Jessie and I came in my car," Kayden said. "What about you guys?"

"We took a cab," Rex said. "Why don't you guys take Kayden's car, and we'll go with Ryker?"

"It's a two-seater," Ryker said. "So, I can only take one person." His eyes moved to mine.

I was too tired to think and solve this problem.

"Rae looks exhausted," Ryker said. "I'll take her while the rest of you take Kayden's car."

Jessie's excited look immediately disappeared. She crossed her arms over her chest and pouted in protest.

"Rae can stay with us," Zeke said. "Rex will go with you."

Ryker met his look while keeping his thoughts behind his eyes.

Zeke did the same.

Now I felt like I had two protective brothers. "Look, I'm too tired for this right now. I'll go with Ryker, and you guys take Kayden's car. End of story." I walked to Ryker, feeling sluggish and groggy.

Rex would normally argue, but he was making an effort to back off. "We'll meet you there." He turned around with the others and headed for the car.

Ryker walked with me, and then he snaked his arm around my waist. "You look like a zombie right now."

"I know…" I leaned into his side and rested my face against his chest.

He chuckled. "You really danced your ass off tonight."

"Yeah, I tend to do that."

"You cold?"

"No, just sleepy." He guided me to his car in the parking lot. When we approached the Lamborghini, I squinted at it. "You drive this?"

"Yep." He hit a button on the passenger door and it moved upward.

I watched it rise. "Whoa…"

He grabbed my hand and helped me inside. "You can buckle up, right?"

"Yeah." I leaned back with my eyes closed and felt for the strap with my hands. When I found them, I buckled them together.

Ryker hit the button, and the door began to close again. After he came around to the driver's side, he started the car and left the parking lot.

I looked out the window for a while until I couldn't keep my eyes open. They closed, and I was too tired to open them again.

"Want to go to my place?"

His place? "Why?"

"It's closer, and there's less walking involved."

I liked the less walking part. But I didn't want to have to leave his apartment the next day and come home. Besides, it was a little weird if I stayed there. "Nah. My place is fine."

***

When I woke up, the door was open and Ryker was helping me out. "Home sweet home."

"Yes. My bed is so close."

He put his arm around my waist and walked me inside the apartment building. "So...are you and Zeke a thing?"

"Me and Zeke?" I blurted.

"Yeah." He walked with me up the stairs to the eighth landing.

"No," I said quickly.

"Really?"

"Yeah."

"It just seemed like something was there."

"He's just protective of me because I'm like a little sister to him."

"And that's it?" He seemed incredulous.

We finally reached my floor. "In case you haven't noticed, I'm very close with my friends."

"And maybe you haven't noticed how close Zeke is to you."

Was I just really tired or did that not make any sense? "What?"

"Never mind." He guided me to my door. "You have the key?"

I stuck my hand into my pocket and searched for it. "Yeah..." My fingers kept searching, but I didn't find it anywhere.

Ryker watched my movements. "Did you lose them?"

"No. I think I forgot them." Why did I have to be so stupid right now?

"That's not good."

"It's okay. Rex will be home in the next half hour. I'll just sleep by the door."

"And you think that's a good idea?" The sarcasm was heavy.

"There aren't too many weirdos in my building. I'll be fine." I slid down to the floor and leaned against the wall. My eyes were lidded. "You can go. You don't have to stay here with me."

Ryker didn't step away, but he pulled out his phone. He made a call, and I guessed it was to Rex. "Hey, how far away are you?"

Rex's voice came over the line. "Like, a zillion hours away. There was an accident on the freeway, and we're stuck in dead traffic."

"Really?" Ryker asked. "Because Rae forgot her key to the apartment. We're standing outside it now."

"Well, it's going to be at least an hour and a half, but I'm guessing two."

"Okay."

The wall wasn't the most comfortable place in the world, but I could sleep there if I had to.

"I'm taking her back to my place. She wants to sleep outside the apartment, but I'm not gonna do that."

"That's fine," Rex said. "I'm sorry my sister is so stupid."

"It's okay," Ryker said with a chuckle. He hung up then stuffed his phone into his pocket. "Did you hear all of that?"

"Yeah."

"Then let's head to my place."

"Ugh..."

He grabbed my hand and helped me up. "I hate to imagine how much worse you are when you're drunk."

"You couldn't handle me."

***

The elevator took us directly to his apartment and into his living room.

"Man, I wish I had that in my apartment."

Ryker chuckled before he guided me inside.

I headed straight for the large couch in front of his TV. There was a blanket just over the back of the couch, and I planned to snuggle with that since Safari wasn't around.

Ryker pulled me away. "Come with me."

"I don't need a guest room. The couch is fine." And it's closer.

Ryker took me into his bedroom, where he immediately started stripping down to his boxers.

"Uh, what's going on here?"

"Shh. Just get into bed." He pulled my shirt over my head then removed my jeans.

I was too tired to care, and he'd already seen me naked so there were no surprises.

He laid me on the bed then pulled the sheets down before he tucked me in.

Once my back was on the mattress, I remembered just how comfortable it was. The sheets were made of silk, and the blankets kept my body warm from the cold that pressed against the windows.

Ryker got into bed with me then pressed his chest against my back. His arm hooked across my chest and reached the opposite shoulder. Without thinking, my hand automatically rested on top of his.

Then I fell asleep.

***

Before I opened my eyes, I knew it was noon. The sun was shining through the windows. It was unusually warm for Seattle. My mind was awake and ready for the day, but I didn't want to move.

Then I remembered where I was.

My eyes opened, and I saw the thick arm wrapped around me. Ryker's gentle breaths fell on the back of my neck. His scent washed over me, and I could feel his chest brushing against my back with every breath he took.

What the hell?

I slowly moved from his arms, wanting to leave without waking him. His arm slid past my body then fell on the bed. I got to the edge and looked around for my clothes. They were missing, and I couldn't believe even my panties were gone.

Why wasn't I wearing them?

Did I sleep with him again?

I was pretty sure I didn't.

Just when I was about to stand up, a strong hand grabbed me by the wrist and pulled me back to bed. I turned over to see Ryker staring at me. His green eyes were dull from sleep. His hair was messy from rolling around on the sheets. The sleepy look in his eyes was sexy. Why didn't I ever look like that when I woke up? "Going somewhere?"

"I was trying to sneak out." I blurted out the truth without thinking about it.

"Without saying good morning?"

"Yep."

He smiled liked he was amused. "Well, I'm glad I stopped you." His arm moved around my waist then he kissed my neck and jawline.

His kisses felt good like last time, but also intrusive. "Whoa, what are you doing?"

He moved his lips to my ear. "What does it look like?" He moved over me and ran kisses along my jaw until he found my lips. He gave me a slow kiss full of purpose.

My logical mind became blurry for a second. "I should go..."

"Or you could stay."

"I must look like Rob Zombie right now." My hair was probably a bed of knots, and my makeup made me a perfect extra on *The Walking Dead*.

"Not at all." He brushed his lips past mine. "You look beautiful." He said it with such sincerity I lost my train of thought. "I like the way you look in the morning."

"You do?" My hands drifted to his biceps, noting the prominent muscles there. I was losing my train of thought again. Ryker distracted me with his pretty words.

"Definitely." He kissed the corner of my mouth and burned me with the heat.

Now all I wanted to do was lie there and enjoy the gorgeous man on top of me. He had everything I could ever want. He was handsome in a classic way, his body was perfect, and he was sweet and reserved at the same time.

But I couldn't go down this path again.

"I should get going. I need some coffee and pancakes." It was Sunday. We always had breakfast at the apartment and watched football, along with playing some board games.

"How ironic," he whispered. "I have both." He didn't get off of me. In fact, he started kissing me again, moving to my neck and chest.

Anytime he touched me, it felt amazing. With just his lips, he could make me writhe. "Ryker, you're super hot, but I can't do this again."

"I'm super hot, huh?" He kissed my stomach.

"Yeah. But it's best if I just leave."

He grabbed my thighs and separated them before be pressed his face between them. Those amazing kisses touched my most sensitive area, and I immediately arched my back and lifted my hips in response.

Ryker kissed and licked the area, giving me the best head I'd ever received. His tongue worked my clitoris before it slipped into my passage.

I writhed all over again. "Oh..."

Ryker kissed me harder, igniting my entire body in flames.

In the back of my mind, I knew I needed to leave. I had to end this. But my body wouldn't listen to me. It was enjoying this way too much.

He rubbed my clitoris with his thumb and cherished the rest of my body with his mouth. His warm breaths fell on the sensitive area, highlighting all the pleasure. He pushed my body and mind to the edge of ecstasy.

I was at the edge and about to fall into sweet oblivion. My body temperature rose a few degrees. My quiet moans turned into screams. My fingers dug into his forearms, and I prepared for an orgasm that burned me with white-hot flames.

Just before I hit my threshold, Ryker pulled away.

"No..."

He crawled up my body, a slight smile on his mouth. His lips were coated with my fluid. They shined like lip gloss. "Stay."

"You're such a jerk." I dropped my head on the pillow with defeat.

"I'll keep doing it if you stay."

My body wanted to give in so I could return to that sweet heaven. Ryker was so good with those damn lips. Where did he learn to do all of that? Oh yeah, all the women he'd screwed over the years. "I want to but...it's not a good idea."

"Yes, it is. It might not be as good as last time. But there's a good chance it'll be even better." He gave me a kiss, wanting me to taste myself. Then he opened the nightstand and pulled out a foil packet.

"No. It was fun as a one-time thing, but we can't keep doing it."

"Why not?" he pressed. "Why can't it be a two-time thing?"

"Because it becomes a slippery slope. It becomes complicated. We'll no longer be friends. We'll be friends with benefits."

"I don't see the problem."

"I don't want that."

He sighed as he looked down at me. "What do you want?"

"I don't know," I said with a shrug. "To be friends."

"Your wet pussy tells me otherwise."

"Well, when you fuck it with your mouth like that, it doesn't have much of a choice."

His eyes darkened at my words. "Sweetheart, I'm not letting you leave until I get what I want." He parted my thighs with his and positioned himself over me.

"Good luck with that." I moved from under him and got to the edge of the bed. I grabbed my clothes and started dressing myself.

He sighed then sat up with his back to the headboard.

I didn't feel bad for him. "Just think about me when I'm gone."

"I definitely will."

I pulled my clothes on then tried to fix my hair.

Ryker left the bed and pulled his sweatpants on. He remained shirtless, his chiseled and hard physique looking particularly nice as it glistened with sweat. He was practically pouting because he didn't get what he wanted.

"Not used to hearing no?"

"Actually, no."

I grabbed my phone from the nightstand.

Ryker came toward me, the determination in his eyes. "Why not? I want you and you want me."

"I told you," I said. "It gets complicated. Feelings get involved and somebody gets hurt— probably me."

"Have you done this before?"

I shrugged. "I don't kiss and tell."

He tilted his head slightly. "And we're supposed to be just friends?"

"Just friends?" I asked. "Friendship is a beautiful thing."

His eyes narrowed on my face.

"If you really want a beautiful woman right this second, I know Jessie would take you in a heartbeat." I felt like a pimp dishing out my friend.

"I don't want her." He said it with such harshness it felt like sandpaper against my skin.

"Why?" I blurted. "She's gorgeous. That's just not possible."

He held my gaze as he spoke. "I've seen better."

Well, he's a freak then. "I should get going." I stepped around him and left the bedroom.

He followed behind me, his large feet hitting the hardwood floor.

I got to the elevator doors. "Well, thanks for letting me crash here."

"You can crash here whenever you want."

And have to battle his kisses before I got out? I resisted him this time, but I didn't think I could do it again.

"Let me drive you home."

"No, it's okay. I'll just walk."

"I really don't mind."

"Neither do I," I said. "You know how committed I am to exercise."

He smiled at my reference. "If you ever want to sleep over with Safari, you're welcome to bring him along."

"Ew, no," I said. "He would get hair everywhere."

"I have a vacuum."

I needed to leave before my vagina started making the decisions. "Well, I'll see you later." I hit the button on the elevator and tried not to scream as the number on the top showed it was on the first floor.

Ryker stared at me with darkly burning eyes, silently convincing me to change my mind.

Speed it up, elevator.

He stepped closer to me, those lips about to go in for the kill.

No. No. No.

I glanced at the elevator. It was only on the fourth floor.

Ugh.

Ryker moved his arm around my waist then pulled me into him.

Just push him off. That's it. Problem solved.

Then he cupped my cheek. "Can I have one to go?"

Fuck it.

He pressed his lips to mine and kissed me slowly.

I kissed him back and loved every second of it. My arms moved around his neck, and my tits brushed against his bare chest. The longing overtook me, and I felt my tongue dance with his. He was such a good kisser, and he constantly made me lose my train of thought. All I thought about was him, this kiss, our bodies—just us.

The elevator beeped when it arrived.

I pulled away but his hold was reluctant. He didn't release me right away, having to force himself to do it.

I stepped into the elevator so he couldn't grab me again. Honestly, I was more worried about jumping back into his arms. "Just friends."

He stood with his hands on his hips, just staring at me.

"You know, platonic friends." I hit the lobby button and anxiously waited for the doors to close.

His eyes narrowed on my face.

"The kind that play board games and stuff." Why the hell wouldn't the damn doors close?

He crossed his arms over his chest.

"Like, we can go to ball games and stuff. Maybe share a hot dog. That's it." I hit the button again to speed things along. "Is your elevator broken or something?"

154

He finally made his move and stepped toward the elevator.

"No!" If he crossed the threshold, I'd be screwed. I hit the door close button and it shut just in time. Ryker was gone from my sight and the elevator started to descend.

Thank god.

***

When I came home, everyone was already there.

Jessie and Kayden were sitting at the kitchen table, breakfast laid out on plates. They both turned to me and looked me up and down, noting my wrinkled clothes and messy bun.

They both gave me that look.

"Is that you?" Rex called from the living room.

"Yeah, I survived." I tossed my purse on the table and walked into the living room. The game was on the TV, and Zeke and Rex were already drinking beer and watching it.

Zeke watched me with concern in his eyes. "Everything okay?"

"Yeah." Why wouldn't it be?

"So..." Rex made an awkward face. "Did you..." He rubbed his chin. "I mean..." He paused again. "Never mind. I have nothing to say."

"Nothing happened." I answered his unspoken question. That wasn't totally truthful because some stuff happened, but we didn't sleep together. I knew that's what both he and Zeke were wondering.

Rex sighed in relief.

Zeke did the same thing.

Why was everyone so interested in my personal life? "Alright. I need breakfast." I headed into the kitchen and made a plate of pancakes, bacon, and eggs. Then I sat at the table with the girls.

Jessie was immediately on me. "Okay. What really happened?"

Kayden leaned forward in anticipation.

"We didn't sleep together." I poured the syrup on my food. "I'm surprised you didn't hook up with him, Jessie. It seemed like you guys were having a good time at the concert."

"He wasn't into me—at all."

"What?" I didn't believe that for even a second.

"Yeah," she said. "He was nice to me and everything, but he wasn't taking the bait. Then I mentioned that you thought he and I would really hit it off. You know, just in case he thought it would be weird to fool around with your friend. But it seemed to piss him off. He didn't say anything else to me for the rest of the night."

My plate of breakfast was untouched. "That doesn't make any sense."

She shrugged. "That's what happened. He was all brooding and quiet. And he kept staring at you."

"He did," Kayden said. "I saw him."

Why wouldn't he sleep with Jessie? She was beautiful with a perfect body. And she basically placed herself on a dish for him.

"When he took you to his place, nothing happened?" Jessie asked incredulously.

"Well...some things happened." I kept my voice quiet so the guys wouldn't hear.

"What?" Kayden pressed.

"I tried to sleep on the couch, but he forced me into his bedroom. Then he took off my clothes and got into bed with me. We just snuggled through the night. But this morning, he was up in my grill. He tried to seduce me, but I managed to get out of there before I lost my resolve."

"Why didn't you let him seduce you?" Jessie asked. "I don't get it."

"I don't want to be in that kind of relationship again," I said. "I'll fall for him, and then he'll toss me aside when he's done with me. It was fun as a one-night stand, but if we keep doing it, I'll become a plaything of his. I'm not going there again."

"I get it," Kayden said.

"He's a player," I said. "And once a player, always a player."

"If he's a player, why didn't he just sleep with me?" Jessie asked.

"Uh…" I didn't have an answer to that.

"She has a good point," Kayden said.

"Maybe he already knew the sex was good, so he wanted to do it again?" I couldn't read Ryker's mind. He was pretty closed off most of the time, so I wasn't going to bother. I didn't have a pickaxe sharp enough.

"I don't know…" Jessie rested her chin in her palm. "Maybe he doesn't want a fling."

"If that were the case, he would have asked me out." And I wasn't going to wait around for that.

"That's true," Kayden said. "So what now?"

"We're just friends," I said. "And we're going to stay that way."

"You really think so?" Jessie asked.

"I told him that's what I wanted," I said. "As long as I'm not alone with him, it shouldn't be a problem."

Rex came into the kitchen to get a new beer. "What are you guys talking about?"

I tried to think on my feet.

"Our favorite romance movies," Kayden blurted.

He twisted the cap off the new bottle and cringed. "Ugh. That's the most boring thing I've ever heard." He walked back into the living room and joined Zeke.

I smiled at her. "Good one."

"I was going to say tampons but that's better," Jessie said. "More believable."

I ate my pancakes then moved on to my eggs. "So, you guys have fun at the concert?"

Ray of Light

Chapter Six

Rex

"The bar should go here." Zeke indicated the corner area of the bowling alley. "It's visible to the entire building and it's convenient."

I nodded. "Yeah, I think that would work."

"I'd put the food court over there," Zeke said. "Keep them separate. You don't necessarily want the drinkers with the eaters. And if we have an arcade, we don't want the kids to be mingling with the wrong crowd."

"True. Since it's a 60s and 70s theme, should we sell weed?"

"You would be asking to get caught, man."

He had a point. "True."

"Rae said she would get estimates from a few contractors. Once that's done, we should be able to move forward."

"Sounds good." I still felt guilty as hell taking anything from Zeke. "Are you sure you want to do this? Because if you change your mind, I'm not going to be upset at all."

He patted my shoulder. "Dude, don't worry about it. Of course I want to help you out."

I would just get a loan from the bank, but my credit was terrible. "Well…thanks."

"You want to get wings and beer?"

"Always."

***

We shared a bucket of fries and wings while we drank our beers. The TV in the corner showed the highlights of the game. The place was fairly quiet because people hadn't gotten off work just yet.

Zeke became particularly quiet, almost brooding. I'd known him for so long and spent so much time with that I could read him like a book. Something was on his mind. "Everything alright, man?"

"Yeah." He took a long drink of his beer.

I kept eating. If he said nothing was wrong, then nothing was wrong. Rae always pestered me until she pulled it out of me. That wasn't my tactic. "That concert was pretty cool. We should do that more often."

"Yeah..."

I was pretty sure I didn't do anything to piss him off, so whatever he was mad about had nothing to do with me. "I need a haircut. I think I'm going to have Jessie do my hair. She'll probably do it for free, especially since I'm broke as hell."

"Good idea."

"I went to the library the other day and saw Kayden. The weirdest thing happened—"

"There's something I need to tell you, and I've been dreading it."

Okay...maybe there was something wrong. "What's up?"

He'd already finished two beers so he was obviously building up to this moment, hoping the alcohol would make it a little easier.

I picked at my fries but didn't eat them because I was anxious to hear whatever he had to say. Zeke and I hung out all the time, but we didn't have many deep conversations. We stuck to sports, sports, and women. Heart-to-heart talks weren't really our thing.

Zeke remained silent, trying to figure out how to start.

"Dude, it's me. You can tell me anything."

"It's different..."

How different could it be?

"You're probably going to be upset with me. That's why I'm hesitant."

"Well, I don't get mad very often, so you're probably exaggerating."

"Uh...I don't think I am."

"It's not like you slept with Rae or something." I chuckled then ate a few fries.

Zeke had a guilty look on his face.

I stopped eating when I caught the look. A fry was about to enter my mouth when I halted. "You didn't sleep with my sister, right?" Because I would rip his head off.

"No, I didn't."

I relaxed.

"But it's in that same category."

Now I was tense all over again.

"I've had a thing for Rae for a while now. It comes and goes but...this time it's not going away." He held my gaze even though he was uncomfortable with the look. "I know this is weird, and I've debated talking to you about it...so now we're here."

My eyes moved to the TV in the corner because I didn't know what else to do. He just hit me with a slab of bricks. I took a second to recover before I looked at him again. "Why are you telling me this?" We swapped stories about chicks we were seeing, but that was just banter. This was different, and I wasn't sure what his point was.

"Rae is going to be swept off her feet eventually...hopefully not by Ryker. I need to make a move before it's too late. So...I wanted to make sure you were cool with it before I did anything."

I nodded in understanding.

"So...are you cool with it?" He was just as uncomfortable with this conversation as I was.

"I don't know."

Zeke stared at me, holding back his thoughts.

"You guys have been friends for so long. If things didn't work out, it would be really awkward."

"I know."

"Not just between you two. But between you and me, me and Rae, even with the girls. Things would never be the same."

He nodded in understanding.

"Is that a risk you're willing to take?"

"I've thought about it a lot."

"And?"

"I feel like if I do nothing, I'll regret it for the rest of my life."

I rested my elbows on the table. "Then you must really like her."

"Sometimes I think she would be the perfect person for me. If I were going to settle down, it would be with her."

Damn. "I had no idea..."

"I'm pretty good at hiding it."

"Yeah...you fooled me."

"So, is it okay if I go for her?"

"You should really think about it first."

"I have," he said. "A lot."

I rubbed the back of my neck. "Honestly, if things work out between you, she couldn't find a better guy."

He nodded. "Thanks, man."

"But I really don't think she feels the same way. I've never gotten that impression from her. You might tell her how you feel, she might reject you, and then it would always be awkward between you. You know what I mean?"

"Yeah."

"So, you should think about that too."

"I don't think she looks at me that way right now, but if I tell her how I feel, she might see me in a different light. And maybe we can go from there."

"Yeah," I said in agreement. "But there's still a lot of risk involved."

"I know," he said with a sigh. "But I don't know what else to do. I've been with tons of other girls, but I keep coming back to her."

"When did this start?"

"Probably three years ago."

My eyes widened.

"I haven't felt this way the entire time. It comes and goes. I date other girls and stop thinking about her. But the second I'm single again, she's on my mind. I'm doomed to repeat the cycle forever."

"That's intense."

"I know. I wish I could stop thinking about her altogether. But at the same time, I don't."

I crossed my arms over my chest because I didn't know what to say to that.

"So, I think I'm going to tell her."

"Okay." I had a feeling this was going to end badly, but I couldn't tell Zeke what to do. "Good luck."

"Thanks," he said. "And thanks for being understanding. I know this is weird for you."

"It is." I wasn't going to sugarcoat it. "When are you going to talk to her?"

"I don't know." He eyed his beer. "I think I need to take some time to prepare for it. I don't have a damn clue what I'm going to say."

"Just be honest. That tends to work well."

"Yeah."

"But be prepared for her rejection. Because it's a really good possibility."

He nodded with a sad look on his face.

"Do you want me to feel her out first? She told me I need to butt out of her personal life, but I can work around it."

"I don't know. If she felt something for me, you're the last person she would tell."

"True. What about the girls?"

"Don't tell them," he said immediately. "They're loyal to her. I don't trust them with this."

"Okay."

"I know I need to say something soon. I'm afraid if I wait too long, she'll find someone else."

"My sister is a catch, so that's always a possibility."

"And I'm afraid that smug bastard might get into her head."

I assumed he was referring to Ryker. "She said there's nothing going on. If that's what she says, then it's the truth."

"Yeah, probably."

I took a long drink of my beer now that the conversation was over. "I wish you all the luck in the world. It would be sick if it worked out because you'd be my brother-in-law someday."

"Yeah, that would be cool."

But that was wishful thinking. If Rae had a thing for Zeke, it would have come up a long time ago. She would have flirted with him or dropped hints. I could read her pretty well, so I would have noticed it.

But I didn't have the heart to tell him that.

***

I opened the front door to see Kayden on the other side. "Hey, what's up?"

The second she saw me, she tensed up. "I'm picking up Rae. We're going shopping."

"Cool." I invited her inside and shut the door behind her. "For slutty lingerie?" I wiggled my eyebrows.

Her entire face turned beet red.

"I'm just kidding..." I didn't mean to offend her.

"I know." She looked even more awkward, standing there and twirling her hair. Then she stared at the ground, growing more uncomfortable by the second.

Why was it always so weird when we were alone together? She was here on Sunday, and there wasn't any weirdness. The concert was fun, and we both had a great time. But when no one else was in the room, it was like nails on a chalkboard.

"So, is Rae ready?" She wore dark jeans that fit dangerously low on her hips. I wondered if her ass would show if she sat down. But she was wearing a long blouse, probably to cover her behind for just those events.

"Actually, she's not home yet."

"Oh..." Panic washed over her face, either because they had an appointment to make or because she would be stuck with me.

I had a feeling I knew which one it was.

"Do you want a beer?" I asked. "Or some water?"

"I'm okay." She continued to stand in one place, not sitting at the kitchen table or on the couch. She'd been here enough times to make herself at home. But she was acting like this was her first time visiting—and we'd never met.

"I've got to ask you something, and I hope you don't take it in the wrong way."

She turned pale as a ghost. It was like looking at Casper. "Okay..."

"Do you have a problem with me?" Maybe she hated me or something. Maybe I did something stupid to offend her and I didn't even realize it. I tend to do that.

"A problem?" she whispered. "No, not at all. I think you're great. Actually, I think you're one of the greatest guys I've ever known. You're so sweet and compassionate, but you're also strong and protective. You look out for the people you care about, and you never expect anything from anyone no matter what you gave them in the past..."

That was one long-ass response. "Thank you."

"I don't have a problem with you, Rex."

"It just seems like..." I pointed between us. "There's something off here, like you're uncomfortable around me or something."

"No, you don't do anything to make me uncomfortable."

"Then what's the deal?" I've seen her with Rae. She was fun and upbeat. She was the same way with Jessie. Sometimes, she was the life of the party. But when it came to just her and me, there was terrible chemistry.

"I..." She shrugged then fidgeted with her hair. "I don't know. I guess you make me nervous."

"Nervous?" I asked. "What? Me?" I was the most easy-going guy in the world. How could I possibly intimidate another person?

"It's not you," she said quickly. "I'm just...a little skittish."

"Around me? We've known each other for ten years. How can I possibly make you feel anything but at ease?" It didn't make any sense to me.

"You know, I don't have an explanation. But I'll be different from now on. How about that?"

I could keep interrogating her, but that wouldn't get me anywhere. If things were going to change, it was best just to focus on that. "That sounds perfect. Let's go out to dinner tomorrow and give it a test run."

"Di-din-ner?" She swallowed the lump in her throat.

"You know, when people get together and eat their last meal of the day."

"I know," she said with a forced chuckle. "I just...never mind. I'd love to go."

I pointed at her. "That's better. Now, we're going to have a good time, and you're going to be comfortable around me. No more of these weird, awkward, tense meetings."

She nodded enthusiastically. "Sounds like a plan. I'm really excited."

That was better. "Okay, I'll pick you up at seven."

"I'll be ready."

Chapter Seven

Rae

I pulled my specimen out of the refrigerator then examined a sample under the microscope. It was only day three of the experiment, and there was significant biodegradable material. The bacteria had eaten away the surface of the plastic and it'd become far more flimsy than before.

My experiment was working.

I wasn't sure how people would respond to it. The fact that bacteria were eating it away would turn off a lot of consumers. But if they knew how much bacteria were in everything they used on a daily basis, they wouldn't blink an eye over it.

I was on to something.

Heavy footsteps sounded behind me, and I knew it wasn't Jenny. "Am I interrupting?"

I didn't need to see his face to know who he was. I recognized his voice the moment he spoke. "No. How can I help you, Mr. Price?" I pulled my gloves off and shoved them into the safety box before I turned to him. I suspected we would run into each other at work sometime, so I was prepared.

He wore a dark blue suit with a gray tie. Like everything he wore, he looked good. Those pretty eyes looked pretty no matter what colors he wore. Even though the suit covered all of his skin, the definition of his arms and shoulders was noticeable.

How did I not sleep with him again? That was a miracle.

"Just came down here to check on things."

"Talk about micromanaging..."

"Or maybe it's just an excuse to talk to you." He came to my side, his arm touching mine.

"I guess I'll never know." I turned away so he wouldn't see how widely I was smiling. The last time I saw him, it was a little awkward. I was practically running from him because it was the only way I could keep my legs closed.

"I'll tell you...one day." He eyed the piece under my microscope. "What are you working on?"

"It was the thing I mentioned before. Things are looking good."

"Want to tell me about it?"

"Would you rather wait until you know if it's even feasible?"

"Hmm... I'm not the kind of person who likes to wait for things."

"You don't say." I didn't keep the sarcasm out of my voice.

He nudged me in the side playfully.

"So, how are things in the big office upstairs?"

"Boring."

I removed my goggles and set them on the counter. "You don't sound particularly passionate about your job."

"What gave me away?" His voice was full of bitterness.

"Then why did you take it?" Did his father make him? I found it hard to believe anyone could make Ryker do anything.

He shrugged but never answered. "I've been thinking about you lately."

"Yeah?" I asked. "In a purely platonic way?"

"Not really…" He gave me a perverted smile.

I swatted his arm playfully. "You're terrible."

"Any exciting plans coming up?"

"Not really," I said. "I've been helping Rex remodel his bowling alley. His business has been scraping by but just barely."

"Yeah, opening a business can be hard."

"Well, he shouldn't have bought it to begin with."

He shrugged. "At least he was trying to invest his money instead of blowing it. Give him some credit."

Everyone defended my brother because they loved him so damn much. "I guess."

"Rex is a pretty cool guy. He was definitely Mr. Popular in high school."

"I'll never understand why."

"I was popular because I'm good-looking. I think he's in the same boat."

"Were you prom king?" I teased.

"No. But I was homecoming king."

I tried not to roll my eyes.

"Were you one of the losers?"

"Pretty much," I said. "I was in academic decathlon, I was the president of the science club, and I played basketball. I was as nerdy as they come."

"Science club?" he asked. "That's actually pretty hot. Wearing your goggles and using a Bunsen burner...sexy."

"Shut the hell up. Stop making fun of me."

"I'm not making fun of you." He came closer to me, his face near mine. "I think you're the sexiest woman in the world." He kept a straight face as he said it. "Why do you think I haven't stopped thinking about you?"

My skin flushed with heat, and I suddenly felt a million degrees warmer. "I should get back to work. I'll give you an update when I have more data."

He seemed disappointed with the brush-off. "I hope I see you soon—and not at work."

"Well, we're playing pool this week if you want to come." I wasn't getting tangled up with him. Last time I was too close to the fire, I got burned.

"Let me ask you something." He walked around me then approached me from the other side, circling me like a shark. "Why won't you be with me?"

"I told you why." I didn't want to keep having this conversation.

"Not really."

"I don't want to have a meaningless fling."

"So, you want a relationship?"

"I guess." Not every guy had to be my future husband, but I didn't want to fool around with a guy when I was absolutely certain it wouldn't go anywhere—and I would fall in love with him. "And you don't do those. That's why it'll never work."

"We can't just have some fun?"

"We already did."

"More fun," he said.

"Our time has run out. But my friend Jessie is interested in you."

His eyes darkened in anger. "I told you I wasn't interested."

"Then Kayden is your next pick."

"She doesn't do anything for me either."

"Geez, you're picky."

"No, I'm really not," he said. "But when I find something I really like, I stick with it." He kept staring at me.

"Ryker, listen to me."

He stood up straight and looked me in the eye.

"The only reason you want me so badly is because you can't have me. I'm not going to change my mind about this. You can keep trying to seduce me all you want, but it won't work. We both want different things in life, so let's just leave it at that."

"Actually, I think we want the exact same thing," he said. "I can give you exactly what you want—night after night."

My thighs screamed in desperation. "More than once leads to emotional attachment."

"Just don't get attached."

Easier said than done.

"You clearly aren't considering the fact that you threw Jessie at me." His voice suddenly became angry, like he was offended I gave my friend permission to pursue him.

"I didn't throw her at you. She was into you, and I told her to go for it."

"Just like that?" he asked incredulously. "You wouldn't have cared if I slept with her?"

"No." I wasn't lying either. "Because we aren't anything, Ryker. We don't mean anything to one another, beyond our friendship. And let's keep it that way. If we keep sleeping together…"

"What?"

"It just…makes things blurry."

"You're afraid you'll start caring about me."

No. I already did care. I was afraid I'd fall in love with him. "Yeah, I guess."

He nodded in understanding.

"You're a pretty man with pretty words. You can have whomever you want. Don't waste your time on me."

"That would be fine if there was someone else I wanted."

I turned to him, confusion sweeping through me. "What?"

He stared at me for several heartbeats, without blinking. The look lasted for ages, practically years. Then he stepped away and headed to the door. "Nothing, Rae. Nothing."

***

I just sat down to dinner with Rex when my phone vibrated. Zeke was calling me.

Rex shoveled an enormous piece of lasagna into his mouth. "Damn, this shit is good."

"You eat food out of the trash, so your compliments don't mean much." I took the call. "Hey, dude. What's going on?"

"When did you start calling me dude?" he asked with a chuckle.

"I guess now." I ate while I talked.

"Who is that?" Rex asked. "Is it Zeke?"

"Mind your own business."

"Excuse me?" Zeke asked.

"Sorry, I was talking to my dipshit brother."

"Oh. Gotcha."

"We're having dinner right now," I said. "Want to come over?"

"No, it's okay," he said. "I already ate. I was wondering if you're free on Saturday for dinner."

"Dinner?" I asked. "With the gang?"

"Actually, I want it just to be you and me."

Zeke and I had done stuff together alone tons of times, but he never asked me to dinner before. Maybe he wanted to talk about something. Or maybe he was just sick of Rex. "Yeah, sure. Sounds good."

"Cool," he said. "I'll talk to you then."

"Alright, see you later, dude."

He chuckled. "Alright, dudette."

I hung up and kept eating.

"So...what did Zeke want?" Rex kept his eyes glued to his food.

"He wants to hang out on Saturday."

"Like...just you two?"

Why was he acting like a weirdo all of a sudden? "Yes. Why?"

He shrugged. "Just curious."

"He wants to go to dinner. I suspect he wants a break from you, so that's why he just invited me."

"Uh, maybe."

"Or maybe he wants to talk about the bowling alley without you being there."

"I guess that's possible."

I reached for the last piece of garlic bread but Rex jacked it. "Hey."

"That's payback for all those mean comments you just made."

"Jerk."

"Like I care. I give jerk a good name."

***

Sometimes Ryker came into my mind, but whenever he did, I pushed the thought away.

181

Anytime we were alone together, the intensity was alarming. It actually burned me.

He had the kind of passion that I wanted in a relationship—particularly in a husband. I wanted someone who could be my best friend but also be my greatest lover. Ryker excelled in one category but failed in the other. He was bad news—to the bone.

But sometimes, my imagination drifted away, and I thought about that hard chest and those washboard abs. There had to be hundreds of women before me. Maybe even a thousand. It didn't make me jealous that I wasn't his only one. But I was sad there would be so many after me. One day, he would probably forget he had sex with me at all.

I was in the lab when Aaron, the delivery guy, came down the stairs and entered the lab. "Any harsh chemicals I should be worried about?"

"Nothing but water."

"But that's not a chemical."

"Technically, it is." Most people didn't know that. Water was the most important component to chemical reactions. Without it, most reactions wouldn't happen.

He was carrying a glass vase with two dozen roses inside. They were beautiful and primed. They smelled like summer, a scent I hadn't inhaled in so long. "Wow. Who sent those to Jenny?"

He set them on the table. "Actually, they're for you."

"Me?" I blurted. The last time someone sent me flowers was...never. "Are you sure?"

"That's what the card says." He pointed to the large envelope pinned into the bouquet.

"Who are they from?" The only person who might send me flowers was my brother...and even that was farfetched.

"I don't know. I was just told to send them down here." He headed back to the door.

"Well, thank you, Aaron."

"Sure."

When he was gone, I grabbed the envelope. The handwriting on the front was strictly masculine, but I didn't recognize it. I opened it up and began to read.

Rae,

I want to share a hot dog at a ball game.

I want to play board games with you.

And I want a date.

Ryker

Ray of Light

Chapter Eight

Rae

Ryker asked me out on a date.

A real one.

Did that mean what I thought it meant?

Or did I need to ask for clarification?

I didn't contact him or ask him about it. I was still processing the note he sent. It was sweet, almost too sweet. Did I misread him? Did he want something more? Or did he just want to give me what I wanted so he could get what he wanted?

I left the roses at the office because I didn't know how to explain them to Rex. He wouldn't jump down my throat about it, but he would still ask. I couldn't lie to him, but I didn't want to tell him about Rex. It was easier not to bring them home at all.

After dinner and watching TV, Safari and I went to bed. I had a queen-size mattress, so the two of us barely fit on it together. There was a lot of cuddling between human and canine. But I was used to it and so was he. Safari made cute noises in the middle of the night, and when he dreamed, he released quiet barks. Sleeping with him was better than most guys I'd been with.

My phone lit up on the nightstand the second I closed my eyes.

Ryker was calling me.

I wasn't even sure how he got my number. I took the call, lying in the dark of my bedroom. "Hello?"

There was a long pause before he spoke. "Got my flowers?"

"I did. At first, I didn't know they were for me. You know, because I used to be a loser."

He chuckled. "They were definitely for you."

"They are very beautiful. Thank you."

"So...you'll go on a date with me?"

"That depends," I said. "Do you want to go on a date with me?"

"If I didn't, why would I have asked?"

"It's just...I thought you didn't do that sort of thing."

He sighed into the phone like this was a conversation he didn't want to have. "I don't."

"Then what does this mean?"

"It means I'm making an exception. There's something about you I just can't stop thinking about. When I'm not with you, I want you. And when I have you, I still want you."

My nipples hardened.

"Can I take you out? We'll do the whole dinner thing."

"And getting to know each other?"

"Yeah," he said. "And I'll even walk you to your door afterward."

"You will?" Now I couldn't stop smiling.

"I'll kiss you goodnight. Then I'll go home."

"Wow, this is getting serious."

He chuckled. "I guess it is. So, you're free on Saturday night?"

Was this really happening? Did this hunk of a man really want to take me on a real date? "I am."

"Great. There's this nice place I want to take you."

"What happened to hot dogs at the ballpark?"

"Would you rather do that?" he asked incredulously.

"Actually, yeah. I'd take ballpark food over fancy stuff any day."

He released a sigh of longing. "Baby, you keep getting better."

"Did you just call me baby?"

"I did. And I'm going to keep calling you that."

"That's awfully possessive."

"Didn't you know?" he whispered. "You're officially mine."

***

"He asked you out on a date?" Jessie moved around my chair, combing my hair and trimming it without even watching what she was doing. She was the best hairdresser in the business, and everything was second nature to her.

"Yeah. He sent me flowers and everything."

"Wow. He's really hooked on you."

"I guess." I tried not to smile, but my lips did it anyway.

Jessie caught the look. "You're so into him."

"I've been into him since the first time I saw him," I said with a sigh. "But I tried to keep him at a distance because I knew he would just break my heart. But now…maybe it could go somewhere."

"It is going to go somewhere."

"You think?" I asked hopefully.

"As long as he isn't doing all of this just to sleep with you again. But that would be really shady."

It would be. "No, he wouldn't do that."

"You're sure?"

"Yeah. He's not that kind of guy." He had a dark exterior and he was rough around the edges, but there was a shining light deep inside his soul.

"Then this is very exciting." She finished the trim then gave me a blowout. When she was done making my hair perfect, she turned off the dryer and ran her fingers through my hair. "Why is he like that anyway?"

"I don't have a clue." I didn't ask, and I didn't want to know anyway.

"You think he has some weird issues?" She cringed. "Because he seems...dark."

"I'm not sure." Maybe he just didn't like to commit to anyone. Maybe he liked to be free all the time. Some men were just like that.

"Well, he'll change for you. It's obvious he's obsessed. Whatever you got going on down there is heaven."

I laughed. "It's nothing special."

"I don't know...it must be." She took off the drape covering my body and the hair fell to the floor. "When is the big night?"

"Satur—shit."

"What?"

"We're supposed to go out on Saturday, but I just remembered I have dinner plans with Zeke." "Cancel," she said. "He'll understand. Anytime there's a possibility of sex, it's okay to bail on a friend."

"No. I don't do that." Zeke had been my friend forever. Guys would come and go, but he would be there for life. That's not how I treat my friends. "I'm just glad I remembered before I did something stupid. Ryker and I can just go out on Friday night instead."

"Seriously, it's Zeke. He won't mind."

"I don't blow off my friends for any guy." I stood up then grabbed my purse from the dresser.

Jessie smiled at me. "I respect that." She gave me a high-five. "Alright. That'll be forty bucks."

"Damn, you're expensive."

She shrugged. "I'm the best."

"Well, don't expect a tip."

"Then don't expect another appointment."

I chuckled then handed the cash over. I tipped her twenty bucks because she deserved every penny. "Thanks, girl."

"You're welcome. He's going to love running his fingers through that hair."

"He won't be running his fingers through anything. He said he would walk me to my door, kiss me goodnight, and then leave."

"Wow." Her jaw dropped. "Who knew a beast could turn into Prince Charming?"

I shrugged.

"What are you going to do about Rex? Tell him?"

Ugh, I didn't even think about that. "Uh…I guess."

"He should be fine with it, right? You guys had that talk."

"But I told him nothing was going on with Ryker. Now that I'm going on a date with him, it seems like I lied."

"Just clarify," Jessie said. "And everything should be fine."

"I just wish I had a normal brother."

"Hey." She pointed at me. "My brother doesn't care whether I live or die. Be grateful for what you have."

"I am. I just wish… I don't know."

***

"You come down here a lot." I was sitting at my computer in the lab, transferring data into my spreadsheet.

Ryker sauntered closer to me, his hands in the pockets of his suit. Today, it was black with a gray tie. A shiny watch was on his wrist. The hair on his jaw had been growing for the past few days. I wasn't sure what I liked more, that look or the cleanly shaved one.

He looked good in anything.

"I guess I like to micromanage." He stopped beside my chair. "What are you working on?"

"Data plotting. It's my favorite part."

"Why is that?"

I patted the armrests of the chair. "Because I get to sit."

He chuckled. "You can't do that when you're getting your hands dirty."

"Nope. Too inconvenient."

He stood there like he had nowhere else to go.

"I wanted to talk about our date on Saturday."

"Me too," he said. "If you want to wear a short dress with heels, I'm perfectly okay with that."

I rolled my eyes even though I didn't mean that. "I'll be in jeans, a t-shirt, and a ball cap—just so you know."

"You'll still look sexy."

Now I tried not to smile. "Anyway, I actually already have plans on Saturday. Can we go out on Friday instead?"

"What plans do you have?"

"Zeke and I are hanging out." How could I have forgotten? In the heat of the moment with Ryker, it slipped my mind.

Ryker didn't move or say a word, but his eyes filled with unspoken fire. "You and Zeke?"

"Yeah."

"You're going on a date with him?" His voice didn't increase in volume, but his tone was blowing out my eardrums.

"No, we're just hanging out. Ryker, I have guy friends. This jealousy thing is really annoying. Just to warn you, I won't put up with it. I suggest you let it go."

"I would if he didn't have feelings for you," he said coldly.

Now he was being ridiculous. "Knock it off. He doesn't see me as anything besides a friend—maybe a sister."

"Are you being serious right now?" he asked. "You really don't see it?"

"See what?"

"The way he looks at you. The way he touches you whenever he gets a chance."

"Friends touch each other." This entire conversation was stupid. "I'm not going to change my relationship with Zeke or stop spending time with him. If it really bothers you that much, then we shouldn't see each other."

He held my gaze without blinking.

"I'm not kidding, Ryker. My friends are everything to me. They are my family."

He finally turned away and rubbed the back of his neck slowly. "Fine." The note of finality in his voice told me he was being sincere.

"Thank you." Now that the argument was over, it was tense between us. "Besides, I thought he was your friend."

"He is," Ryker said. "We were pretty close in high school."

"Then you know he's a good guy. I don't have to vouch for him."

He was quiet for so long that it seemed like the conversation was over. "All's fair in love and war."

***

I decided not to tell Rex about Ryker until after the date. Maybe we would spend real time together and realize it would never work. Why get my brother worked up over something that might burn out the moment it was lit?

Fortunately, Rex was working at the bowling alley that night, so I didn't have to worry about the two of them crossing paths. I wore exactly what I told Ryker I was going to wear, and when he picked me up, he looked me up and down and smiled.

"Sporty Spice."

I chuckled. "Yeah, I guess that's the look I'm going for."

"Well, I think you look pretty cute." He grabbed the bill of my hat and lifted it slightly so he could get a better look at my face. "So…do I have to wait until the end of the night to give you that kiss?"

If he kissed me now, we would just go into my bedroom and get busy. "What would a true gentleman do?"

His eyes darkened in disappointment. "I don't remember claiming I was one."

"But tonight you are, right?"

He readjusted my hat on my head. "Unfortunately."

I locked the door behind me and walked with him.

"Rex isn't home?"

"He's working."

"So, he was cool with this?"

"Uh…I didn't tell him."

Ryker stopped walking. "Why not?"

"I'd just rather wait until the last possible moment."

"Because?"

"It's hard to explain." Rex and I had an unusual relationship, but that was because we had such an unusual childhood. No one else understood it but us.

"So, am I a dirty secret? Because I'm okay with that if we're getting dirty."

"No, you aren't a secret," I said. "I'll tell him later."

"When's later?"

"I don't know...tomorrow." Or maybe not.

"I have to say, I've never met a pair of siblings like the two of you."

"I'm sure you haven't."

We headed to the street and reached his car.

"The Bat Mobile."

He stopped and looked at me. "Did you just call my car The Bat Mobile?"

"Well, it reminds me of it."

He chuckled then opened the door for me. "Baby, you keep getting better."

***

"That's the biggest hot dog I've ever seen." Ryker eyed the chili dog in my tray. It was the monster size, full of chili, cheese, peppers, and onions.

"I didn't eat anything all day so I could enjoy this."

"I'm just surprised you can fit that thing into your mouth."

"It's tough at first, but I eventually get it in."

His eyes immediately darkened.

I didn't realize how that could be taken until I already said it.

We were sitting in the second level of the bleachers. Since it was a Friday game, the crowd wasn't as big. And we got pretty good seats for dirt-cheap. Ryker wore jeans and a t-shirt, and his nice arms were noticeable.

I lifted the hotdog and got it into my mouth. I had to take a big bite because if I took little ones, the whole thing would fall apart. There was a specific art when it came to consuming a ballpark hot dog.

Ryker watched me the whole time, examining every move I made. Silently, he watched me eat the entire thing, from one end to the other.

"Damn, that was good." I wiped my mouth with a napkin and felt the burn of the peppers.

Ryker adjusted the front of his jeans. "That was just mean."

"What?"

"You want me to be a gentleman, but you put on that little show? That's like waving a treat in front of a dog even though you know he can't have it."

"I'm sorry you misinterpreted everything. I was just eating my dinner."

"You're the biggest tease I've ever met."

"Am not."

He stared forward and watched the game. "Whatever."

I leaned toward him and moved my hand up his thigh. My lips slowly moved to his ear, and I pressed a kiss against the shell. "I can't wait until I have you in my mouth. I'm sure you'll taste much better than that chili dog." I slowly pulled away, taking my hand with me.

His breathing changed, increasing in pace. When he looked at me, there was a whole new expression on his face. It looked like he wanted to grab me by the back of the neck and drag me out of there.

"Now, that was a tease."

He flared his nostrils then growled.

"Did you just growl at me?"

"Yes, I fucking did." He grabbed me by the back of the neck and yanked my lips against his. The kiss was hard, practically violent. He crushed his mouth against mine and silently told me all the things he wanted to do to me. He sucked my bottom lip with perfect precision before he pulled away. "This gentleman thing is getting old."

"Technically, I never asked you to be a gentleman."

He eyed my lips for a full minute before he met my gaze. "But you asked for something more."

When I looked into those beautiful green eyes, I knew I was slipping away. I wanted more—a lot more. I'd successfully kept my heart locked away for so long, but now the seal on my chest was cracked. "That doesn't mean we can't get dirty too…"

He leaned close to me like he was going to kiss me again. Instead of pressing his lips to mine, he rested them against my ear. He took a deep breath like he was battling something deep inside himself.

I wasn't sure what he was doing, but I liked being this close to him. It was intimate affection without kissing or touching.

"We'll get so dirty," he said. "Filthy, actually. But we'll keep tonight holy—this one time." He kissed my ear, and I could hear the sound of his lips and his tongue. He pulled away, his dark eyes still on me.

The fact he wasn't giving in just made me want him more.

And I didn't even know that was possible.

***

Ryker drove back to my apartment. The radio wasn't on, and only the sound of his powerful engine could be heard in the car. All the lights of his dashboard shined and illuminated his face.

I stuck to my side of the car and tried not to think about his naked body on top of mine. All I wanted was to roll around with him, to feel the sheets cling to the sweat on my back. Heat, passion, and lust consumed me. But since I wasn't getting laid tonight, I had to stop thinking about it.

Ryker kept his eyes on the road but discreetly grabbed my hand. He did it so smoothly, it was like he didn't do it at all. His large hand cupped mine. His strong pulse could be felt through my fingertips. Heat flushed through my skin, making me think about those sticky sheets again. "Thank you for going to the game with me."

"Thank you for taking me."

His eyes were glued to the road but I knew they wanted to look at me. "No more pimping me out to your friends, alright?"

I smiled. "Okay."

"Because neither one of them is my type."

"How is that possible?" Jessie was a brunette and Kayden was a blonde. And they were both stunning.

He shrugged. "I guess I only have one type at the moment."

Like a schoolgirl, I blushed. Thankfully, it was dark in the car so my embarrassing reaction couldn't be seen.

"No more dates."

"This is already exclusive?" I wanted to be exclusive, but I was surprised he demanded monogamy first.

"We're dating, aren't we?"

"That doesn't necessarily mean you don't see other people."

"Well, I don't want you to see other people. I'm guessing you don't want me to see other people."

Not even a little bit. "No."

"Then that's settled." He pulled off the freeway and made it to the city streets. "How's your mom?"

The unexpected question caught me by surprise. I wasn't even aware that he knew who my mom was. "Uh...she's been gone almost ten years now."

Ryker didn't react overtly, but after a few seconds, he released a quiet sigh. "I'm sorry. I didn't know."

"It's okay."

"Rex never mentioned it."

"She passed away after you moved to New York. That's probably why you didn't know."

"What happened? If you don't mind me asking?"

It was a sad story, and I didn't like telling it. "She struggled with depression for a long time. My dad left us when we were young, and she never recovered from it. One day, we came home and found her on the floor with an empty bottle of painkillers beside her."

"Shit," he whispered. "I'm sorry."

"It's okay," I said. "Rex was eighteen and I was fifteen. Since he was a legal adult, he became my guardian and took care of us. It was difficult because he didn't know what he was doing. Until that point, he was enjoying his freedom and doing whatever he wanted. We struggled for a long time."

He nodded slowly. "Everything is starting to make more sense now..."

"Rex still sees himself as my guardian even though I'm old enough to take care of myself."

"And that's why you're so lenient about it." He nodded again. "I understand now."

"Yeah..."

He squeezed my hand and brushed his thumb across my skin.

That affection was enough to make me feel a little better.

***

Ryker walked me to the door, his hand still in mine. "I had a great time."

"I did too."

He faced me then placed his arms around my waist. He looked down at me with longing in his eyes. He slowly pressed his forehead to mine and rested it there. Silence passed for minutes. It was clear Ryker didn't want to leave.

I didn't want him to go either.

He squeezed the small of my back. "I want to sleep with you."

I knew what he meant. "I do too."

"I'm not much of a snuggler, but I like to cuddle with you."

"Well, I went to school for it and everything..."

A slight smile crept onto his lips. "I guess this is where I say goodnight."

"Yeah..." I didn't want to lie in my bed all alone. I wanted this strong man beside me, to kiss my shoulder in the morning then bury his face in my neck. I wanted good sex, all night long.

He leaned in and gave me a closed-mouth kiss on the lips. It was simple and restrained, the most boring kiss we've ever had. He pulled away quickly, like he was kissing an aunt.

I raised an eyebrow. "What the hell was that?"

"I can't give you a real kiss right now," he said. "Because I know what will happen."

"So you give me a granny kiss?"

"A granny kiss? What's that?"

"The kind of kiss you give your grandmother."

"Uh, thanks," he said sarcastically.

"Well, it was."

"You know I'm a damn good kisser. But if I let myself get carried away…" He eyed the wall next to my front door. "I'm going to pick you up and fuck you right there. So, a G-rated kiss is all you're getting."

"That doesn't sound so bad…"

He growled in my face. "Why are you making this so difficult for me?"

"You're the one who decided to be a prude."

"I'm just trying to get you to be mine. You said you wanted something more, so I'm giving you a date. This is what people do on dates."

"And then they screw afterward. That's the whole point of the date."

He closed his eyes for a moment in an attempt to restrain himself. "On our next date, I'll fuck you so hard you won't be able to walk. Alright?"

My core tightened in longing. "When's that gonna be?"

"It could be tomorrow, but you're going out with Zeke." His tone changed noticeably.

"Well, I can come over afterward…"

"After you go out to dinner with him?" he asked. "No, thanks."

"Don't be like that." I met his glare with my own. "I told you this is non-negotiable."

"You know, I really hate it when women tell me what to do."

I crossed my arms over my chest. "Well, you aren't going to like me very much."

He stared at me for several heartbeats. "Actually, I think that is why I like you—in a complicated way." He kissed me on the cheek before he stepped back. "Goodnight, Rae."

I knew I wasn't going to get my way, so I let it go. "Goodnight, Ryker."

"Sweet dreams," he said. "I hope you think of me."

I knew I would be thinking of him—very soon.

***

I tossed and turned and couldn't get to sleep. I kept thinking about those soft lips kissing my body. The way he kissed my ear made my hair stand on end. I wanted Ryker, and my mind couldn't stop thinking about it.

Neither could my body.

I grabbed my vibrator out of the nightstand and didn't feel any guilt as I did it. Just before I turned it on, my phone rang.

I stared at the screen and saw Ryker's name. Maybe he was at my front door because he changed his mind. That would be the greatest news ever. "Hello?"

His breathing was heavy, like he was doing something other than lying in bed. "I want my big cock in that pretty little mouth of yours." The sound of a lubricated hand moving quickly was heard through the phone.

His first words told me everything I needed to know, and they turned me on like crazy. I turned on my vibrator and pressed it tightly against my clit. The vibration immediately got me wet, wetter than I already was. We were strong enough to walk away from each other tonight, but we both gave into the temptation anyway. "Then put it in."

Chapter Nine

Rex

Kayden opened the door.

And my jaw dropped.

She wore a skin-tight black dress with silver heels. Her long legs looked super long in the short dress. Her slim and toned thighs almost looked fake because they were shaped so perfectly.

Her hourglass figure was highlighted in the slim fabric. Her hips were wide and they led to a tiny waist. Up farther, she had a boobalicious chest. I'd always thought Kayden was pretty but tonight...damn.

Her blonde hair was in luscious curls, the kind I liked to fist when I was screwing a girl from behind. She wore light makeup, and the enhancement brought out her blue eyes and full lips.

Fuck.

Kayden watched my expression, her eyes glowing with something I couldn't identify. "Hi."

"Hi..." I couldn't stop staring at her legs. Had they always been that sexy? How did I not notice that before? Was Kayden always this hot? Was it just because she curled her hair? "You look...wow."

"Thanks." Her face turned crimson. A tomato couldn't even compete with her.

I stepped back and allowed her to lock the door. When she was turned around, my eyes immediately went to her legs and her ass.

That was nice too.

"Ready to go?" She turned around, her clutch tucked under her arm.

I needed to adjust my jeans because my dick was getting in the way, but I couldn't do that in front of her. "Yeah, let's go."

***

We sat at the bar. People chitchatted quietly around us and classical music played overhead. The place was crowded but the background noise was at a minimal volume. I preferred regular bars with cheap booze, but since she was dressed like that, I thought we should come here instead.

Her legs were crossed and pivoted toward me on the stool.

I kept glancing at her legs uncontrollably. Knock it off, man. She's like your sister. "How was work?"

"Good," she said. "It was pretty slow, but I like it like that."

"So you don't have to do anything?"

"No. So I can read."

"Gotcha."

"Plus, it's quiet."

I shook my head. "I don't think I could handle all the quiet. It would drive me crazy. Hearing the bowling balls crash against the pins every ten seconds is soothing for me at this point."

"Really?" She smiled like she was enjoying the conversation. "That would give me a headache."

"I just like to be around people—be around life."

"I'm too shy for that."

"That's not true," I said. "I've seen you with Jessie and Rae. The three of you are trouble."

"Well, that's different," she said. "They're my best friends. I can do anything with them."

"I guess I feel that way with Zeke." But there wasn't something I did with him that I wouldn't do with anyone else.

"How's the bowling alley?"

"Still a mess," I said. "I have two employees."

"Are you one of the two?" she asked with a smile.

"Actually, I'm the third employee. But I have a feeling I'm going to have to cut someone soon."

"Hopefully things turn around with all the changes."

"Yeah, but that'll take a while. I'm really lucky Zeke and Rae are willing to help me."

She sipped her drink then returned it to the counter with nothing but grace. "They love you."

"Yeah, I know. Sometimes I wonder why."

"Because you're a sweet person, Rex."

I always got the most compliments from Kayden. She said nice things to me almost every time I saw her. Everyone else made fun of me whenever they had the chance. "Thanks."

"Rae told me your conversation about her personal life went well."

"Yeah...that was a bit awkward. But we got through it."

"She said you've been sticking with it." She stirred her drink before she took another sip. "That's good."

"I slip up sometimes," I said. "I'm so used to asking where she's going and who she's with...like a parent. She's been through a lot, and I can't let her get hurt again. It's not a protective brother thing. It's a family thing."

"I get that."

"The thing about Rae is, she's really confident. That's not a bad thing. But sometimes, she thinks she's stronger than she really is. I'm afraid she'll take on more than she can handle, and when the load is too heavy, she'll collapse."

"I know exactly what you mean."

"I hate being the voice of reason in her head, but I have to do it."

"She appreciates it, Rex."

I felt like we talked about my sister a lot. I reminded myself of a parent who couldn't stop talking about their kids. When my mom passed away, it forced me to be an adult. Since I had to take on that role so quickly while having a teenage girl to look after, it's been ingrained in me ever since. "I wish arranged marriages were still a thing."

"Why?" she asked with a laugh.

"I could go out and find the right guy for her, and then I would be done."

She chuckled. "Rae will find Mr. Right on her own."

"I don't know...she's brought home a lot of losers."

"You think every guy is a loser."

I didn't think Zeke was. Truthfully, Zeke was the best person for her. He could take care of her, talk her down when she was worked up over something, and he would always respect her and treat her right. More importantly, he would make her happy. But I had a feeling they were never going to end up together so I shouldn't waste my hopes and dreams on it.

"Do you think Rae will be that way when you start seeing someone?"

"Ha," I said sarcastically. "No. Rae doesn't care. She knows I can look after myself."

"So...have you been seeing anybody?"

"I hooked up with this girl at the bowling alley. That's about it."

"Oh..." She looked down at her drink. "Recently?"

"Yeah, it was just the other day. We started flirting at the counter, and before I knew it, we were screwing in the men's bathroom. Then she left." There wasn't a single romantic aspect to it. We both just wanted to get laid, even if it was against the bathroom stall.

Kayden stirred her drink, her eyes downcast.

I eyed her, noticing the sudden change of mood. "Did I say something?"

She shook it off. "No, no. I was just thinking about something I forgot to do at work..."

"Screw a guy in the bathroom?" I teased.

She forced a laugh but it was clearly fake.

"Not really your thing?"

"Not so much."

I never talked to Kayden about her personal life, so I didn't really know anything. "Are you the hit-it-and-quit-it kind of girl?" She never had a boyfriend, so I assumed that must be the case.

"No." She shook her head quickly. "No, definitely not."

"Then do you date on the down low?"

"Uh...sometimes."

Did she have an active personal life at all? She was way too pretty not to get offers left and right. Maybe she felt uncomfortable talking about it with me, which was why she wasn't saying much. Was I repeating the same mistakes I made with my sister? "See any good movies lately?"

"I saw *The Revenant*. I really liked it."

"With Leo?" I asked. "I've been meaning to see it."

"You should. It's your kind of movie."

"How do you know what kind of movies I like?"

She shrugged. "I just know what you're into."

We continued talking about music and movies for the next hour. She was more relaxed around me than she usually was, so we were definitely making progress. I'm glad I said something because it was too tense for my liking. It actually felt like we were friends—finally.

"Excuse me," she said. "I'm going to powder my nose."

"What?" I blurted.

"It means I'm going to the bathroom."

"Oh." I nodded. "That was too classy for me to understand."

She gave me a smile before she walked away. Instantly, all heads turned her away, admiring her perfect physique and gorgeous legs.

I wasn't ashamed to admit it. I stared at her ass the entire time.

"Excuse me?" A feminine hand gripped my shoulder.

"What's up?" I turned in her direction and saw a cute brunette. She was tall for a woman, just less than six feet.

"Are you with anyone?"

"No. I'm just hanging out with my friend." I looked her up and down and liked what I saw. "See something you like?"

She smiled. "I do, actually. My name is Reina."

"Hey, Reina." I shook her hand. "I'm Rex."

"It's nice to meet you." She stood there like she expected me to offer her a drink.

"I'd love to chat, but I don't want to ignore my friend. Can I have your number so I can give you a call later?"

"That sounds perfect." She wrote her number down on the napkin.

"I look forward to it." She flipped her hair over one shoulder as she walked away.

I watched her go, wondering what kind of kink she was into.

Just when she was gone, another girl came up to the pitcher's mound. "Sorry to bother you, but I think you're really cute."

"Who doesn't?" I smiled and shrugged at the same time. "And what a coincidence. I think you're cute too."

She chuckled. "What are the odds?"

"I'm actually with a friend right now, so I'm not available for chitchat. Can I have your number so I can call you later?" I just hoped I didn't get her mixed up with the other girl.

"That sounds great." She grabbed a napkin and scribbled her number down. She also added her name.

I read her name out loud. "It's nice to meet you, Hannah. I'm Rex."

"It's nice to meet you too. I hope I can get to know you better."

"I have a strong feeling you will."

She gave me a sweet smile before she walked away.

Damn, I'm awesome. I didn't even have to put the moves on anyone tonight. They just flocked to me.

Kayden came back from the bathroom, attracting the attention of the entire bar as she walked. She returned to the stool and set her clutch on the counter. "Hope you weren't too bored while I was gone."

"Actually, I wasn't." I held up the two napkins. "I scored two numbers. Pretty slick, huh?"

She stared at the napkins like they were two insects. Almost immediately, she became tense all over again. Eye contact was broken, and she fidgeted with her clutch. "I just realized I need to get home."

What? We'd only been here for an hour. We didn't even get to dinner yet.

"It was nice seeing you, Rex. I'll talk to you later." She stood up and left the stool.

"Whoa, what? Are you mad or something?"

"No," she said quickly, still not looking at me. "I just remembered...I have to feed my dog."

Her dog? "You don't have a dog."

"I'm watching it for a friend." She walked away without even saying goodbye to me.

What the fuck?

I watched her go, trying to figure out what just happened. She went to the bathroom and everything was fine. But as soon as she started talking to me, she flipped out and left. What was I missing?

I went after her and followed her to the sidewalk. She was heading to her apartment to the left.

I caught up to her. "Kayden, hold on."

She kept walking. "I'll talk to you later, Rex. I'm in a hurry right now."

"Just talk to me. Did I do something? Say something?" I got tired of her ignoring me, so I grabbed her by the arm and forced her to stop in her tracks. "Kayden, talk to me."

When her face was visible, her eyes were full of tears. Her cheeks were blotchy and red, and her chest was expanding at an alarming rate.

In shock, I just stared at her. "I don't know what I did to upset you, but I'm sorry."

"It's not you." She pulled away and sniffled. "Just let me go." She twisted out of my grasp and kept walking.

I should have gone after her, but I didn't. Not once in my life did I understand women. It was a science I never studied. But never in my life had I been more confused than I was right then.

What just happened?

***

I walked in the door feeling like shit. I tossed my keys on the table, but they slid across the surface and fell to the floor.

I didn't bother picking them up.

Rae was Kayden's best friend, so I decided to ask her about it. Maybe I did something incredibly offensive, and I didn't even realize it. I needed the help of another woman for this one.

Rae came down the hall, dressed to go out. "Hey. I need to talk to you."

"That's perfect because I need to talk to you too."

Her purse was over her shoulder, and her hair was in curls. "Okay, I know this is strange, but just bear with me."

Could my night get any worse?

"When I told you nothing was going on between Ryker and me, I meant it. That was the truth. We were just friends who had an attraction to each other. I didn't want to get involved with him because he's a manwhore. But he asked me out the other day, and I said yes. We went to a ballgame and had a great time. Since we hit it off so well, I'm going to see him again."

Kayden left my mind immediately. "Whoa...hold on." That was a ton of information to get in thirty seconds. "So, you're dating Ryker now?"

"Yes."

That was my worst nightmare. "No. Rae. No."

She raised an eyebrow.

"He's the biggest player I know. He's worse than me, if you can imagine it. He's not good enough for you, and he never will be. He's just going to break your heart. Just trust me on this."

She crossed her arms over her chest. "What did we talk about, Rex?"

"I know. I know." I raised both of my hands in frustration. "I'm not trying to stick my nose where it doesn't belong, but I need to warn you. He might be a smooth talker, but he's just trying to get into your pants."

"Rex, I'm a big girl, and I can make my own decisions."

"I'm just trying to save you some time and heartbreak."

"Ryker asked me out on a date—a real one. This isn't a fling."

"That's what he wants you to think." Ryker was a good guy, in general. But I didn't want him with my sister.

"He's different with me."

I rolled my eyes. "Every guy is different with you. But then they all end up showing their true colors."

She stomped her foot. "Rex, I'm not asking for your permission. I'm just telling you what's going on. Don't get those two things mixed up."

"I really, really think this is a bad idea."

"Well, I don't care what you think. I really like him, and I want to be with him."

God, this was terrible.

"So, just let it go."

I wanted to keep arguing, but would that do me any good? "Don't expect me to comfort you when he breaks your heart, Rae. Because I won't." I saw the ending before it even began. She would fall in love with him, and he would move on with a supermodel. I'd seen it enough times.

"You haven't seen him in ten years. You don't even know what he's like anymore."

"I know he hasn't changed."

"Whatever." She held up her hand to silence me. "You can bitch and moan all you want, but it's not going to change anything."

"Fine. Go waste your time. See if I care."

"I don't." She stomped her foot again.

The doorbell rang.

My eyes immediately went to it, and the rage kicked in. "Is it him?" It would be the perfect opportunity to rip his head off.

"It's Zeke."

The anger immediately died down. "Zeke?"

"We're going to dinner tonight." She opened the door and greeted him. "Hey. Are you as hungry as I am?"

Shit. Today was Saturday.

She was having dinner with Zeke.

And he was going to tell her about his feelings.

Fuck, he was going to get demolished. "Zeke, I need to talk to you for a second." I wasn't going to let my friend make an idiot of himself. He would never recover from that.

"No." Rae grabbed his arm. "We're already running late, and you two talk forever like a bunch of schoolgirls."

Zeke chuckled. "She has a point, man."

"No, this is damn important." I grabbed his other arm.

"Rex." Rae pushed me off. "Not now. I already know what you're going to say, and I don't have time for it." When she grabbed Zeke, he immediately let her pull him along because he was whipped like a damn pussy.

"Zeke." I followed him out the door then I made a gesture with my hand that said, "Don't tell her."

He tilted his head to the side. "What?"

"Rex, what are you doing?" Rae asked.

I ignored her. "Dude, don't do the thing you were gonna do. You know what I'm talking about?"

Zeke still looked confused. "Uh..."

"Just don't do the thing you were going to do," I said firmly. "Abort it." I hoped he would understand I was telling him this for a reason, not just because I didn't particularly like it.

"What thing?" Rae asked. "Rex, what are you talking about?"

"Trust me," I said to Zeke. "Don't. Do. It."

"Zeke, what's he talking about?" Rae asked.

Zeke's eyebrows furrowed. "I'm not sure..."

"Well, let's go." Rae started to walk away. "I'm starving."

Zeke gave me a confused look before he walked away.

I had a feeling this was going to be a disaster. I pulled out my phone and sent him a text message. He would probably check it sometime before they had dinner. *Dude, don't tell her how you feel. She just told me she's dating Ryker and she's really into him. I'm sorry, man.*

Poor guy.

Ray of Light

Chapter Ten

Rae

"Would you judge me if I got the ribs?"

Zeke looked at me from across the table, the corner of his lip upturned in a smile. "Do I ever judge you for anything?"

"True. That's why we're friends." I closed the menu because I knew exactly what I wanted.

"I'm sure there's more to it." He set his menu down.

After the waiter brought our drinks and took our order, we were alone again. I couldn't stop thinking about that conversation Rex just had with Zeke. "So, what was that weird thing back at the apartment?"

"With Rex?"

"Yeah."

He shrugged. "You know Rex. Scientists have been studying him for years, and they still don't understand him."

I laughed. "Yeah, I guess that's true."

"How's work?"

"Good. I'm working on that biodegradable packaging project, and I've seen good results."

"That's awesome," he said. "If it works out, it could really change the consumers' habits."

"I know. I'm just worried it won't be convenient enough. We live in a world where most people get their nutrition through the drive-thru and microwave dinners. This might be too much for them."

He nodded. "I see what you mean. But there's a large population of people in the U.S. that really care about recycling and protecting the environment. You'll appeal to them."

"True."

"I think it's great what you're doing, Rae. It really makes a difference." He held my gaze without blinking.

He always gave me looks like that, like he was fond of me or proud of me. He was a mix between a best friend and a brother. Sometimes I felt more comfortable telling him things than Jessie and Kayden. Zeke and I clicked the moment we crossed paths. It just felt right with him. "Thanks."

He sipped his beer but continued to look at me. "How's the office?"

"Good. I had a patient with severe cystic acne. It was the worst I've ever seen. Over the course of three months, I've been treating it with antibiotics, topical cream, and a specific moisturizer. It's done wonders. When she came in the other day, she started crying because her face had improved so much."

"Awe…"

Emotion was in his eyes. "Yeah…I love my job."

"That's so great for her. Is she young?"

"Sixteen."

"Oh, so that's a really big deal."

"It is," he said. "She's a pretty girl, so she's going to have a lot of self-esteem now."

"That's great."

"Her parents didn't have good insurance, so they couldn't afford most of the medications. So I didn't charge her for my time."

That didn't surprise me at all. "You're so sweet, Zeke. If I were sick, I'd want you to take care of me."

He smiled. "I would always take care of you, Rae."

Our conversation was interrupted when the food arrived. My baby back ribs looked messy, and his chicken looked elegant.

Zeke eyed my food. "Should I ask for extra napkins?"

"That would probably be best."

He waved down the waiter.

Once I had them, I set them right next to me. I'd definitely need them for this meal. "Seeing anybody?" Zeke didn't usually have girlfriends, at least serious ones. He'd see someone for a few weeks before he moved on to someone else.

"Not right now."

"Taking a break?" I asked. "Need to recuperate?" He told me about this sex addict he was seeing. It was fun at first until his dick felt sore.

He chuckled. "Yeah, I guess." He looked down at his food as he ate.

I should tell him about Ryker since he would hear about it from my brother. And I'd rather have Zeke hear the real story of what happened rather than the ridiculous one my brother made up.

"Speaking of seeing people..." He stopped eating altogether and set down his fork. "There's something I want to talk about, and it's not exactly easy." He rubbed the back of his neck and didn't make eye contact with me for a long time.

Seeing Zeke nervous about anything wasn't normal. He was always confident and good with words. My phone vibrated on the table and lit up. I felt rude looking at it when Zeke was trying to tell me something important so I ignored it.

Zeke glanced at it. "It's okay."

I quickly checked it.

It was a message from Ryker. *Just dinner. No touching.*

I rolled my eyes and set the phone down again. Ryker wasn't even my boyfriend, and he was already annoying me.

"Everything okay?" Zeke asked.

"Yeah, it's nothing. What were you saying?" I took a bite of my mashed potatoes.

He paused again before he started up. "I've been feeling this for a long time, and I've debated telling you. It could make you uncomfortable, but I hope it doesn't because it could also lead to great things so I feel like I should tell you. If I don't say anything, I'll regret it—"

My phone lit up again.

Goddammit, Ryker.

Zeke halted and stared at it. "It's okay." He wasn't the kind of person to get mad at anything for any reason. He was laid back and mellow.

"I'm sorry. I'll just turn it off." I grabbed the phone and read the message. *Come over afterward. I want to kiss every inch of you until his presence his gone.*

He really was ridiculous.

I turned off the phone and shoved it into my purse.

"May I ask what that's about?" Zeke asked. "Is it important?"

"No, not important at all." If Ryker weren't so damn hot and sweet, I wouldn't put up with it. "It's just Ryker, being...Ryker."

Zeke held my gaze, but his look slightly changed. His seriousness ebbed away and was replaced with intensity. Thoughts ran through his mind. I could see it on the surface of his eyes but couldn't make out exactly what those thoughts were. "You and Ryker talk a lot?"

"Well...it's a long story. I'll tell you when you're done."

Zeke didn't finish his story. He dropped it entirely. "When you say it's a long story, does that mean you're seeing him?" He swallowed the lump in his throat, and the usual confidence in his look and frame disappeared.

"Actually, yeah."

He didn't react at all. He stared at me blankly, his entire body rigid. Then his eyes slowly started to drift down until he was staring at the surface of the table. He closed his eyes and breathed a deep sigh.

"Don't tell me you're against this too," I said. "I just told Rex at the apartment, and he acted like it was the worst thing in the world."

Zeke rubbed his temple.

"When we first met in the park, there was obvious chemistry there. When we met again, the sparks flew all over again. We hooked up, and it was really great. But I moved on after that because I knew what kind of guy he was." I wouldn't tell any of this to Rex because it was just awkward, but Zeke and I told each other everything. He knew what to filter out when he spoke to my brother. "But then we started working together and spending more time together. He asked me out the other night and I said yes. The rest is history. I don't know what it is about him, but I really like him. He makes me feel...alive. You know?"

Zeke hadn't looked at me once. He was still rubbing his temple like he was fighting off a migraine.

"Zeke?"

He sat up straight and dropped his hand. "Yeah, that's great. Ryker is a bit of a ladies' man, but I'm sure you know that."

At least he was being supportive about it, unlike Rex. Rex never thought anyone was good enough for me. "Yeah. I'm not going into this as an ignorant person. I understand the risks, but I think everything will be fine."

He grabbed his fork and poked at his food. The atmosphere around him was bleak and dark. He slouched at the table, his shoulders coming down and his back arching. He didn't look like himself at all.

"Zeke?"

"Hmm?" He flicked his chicken around.

"Is there something wrong?"

"No, not at all."

He never lied, but I got the distinct impression he wasn't being truthful. "Are you sure?"

"Yeah…" He shook his head as he stared off into the distance. "I just…never mind."

"What?" I pressed.

"It's nothing. It's something that happened at work…not worth mentioning."

"Okay." I dropped the subject because it didn't seem like he wanted to discuss it. "What were you going to say?"

"Oh…yeah." He set his fork down again. "I've been doing a lot of thinking about Rex's bowling alley."

Did he want to pull out of the investment?

"I think I should invest all the money. I already own a house and a business. You should save your money for a house or something."

That was what he wanted to talk about? He made it seem like something serious was going on. "Zeke, it's really okay. I wouldn't have offered if I wasn't financially able to handle it."

"But there's a chance you could lose all that money."

"I'm okay with that," I said. "I really want to make this work for my brother. I'm not sure what else he would do, you know? I can tell he's always felt a little lost."

He nodded. "I know what you mean."

"So, it's fine. Don't worry about it."

"Okay." He kept his head down as he ate.

The conversation was a lot tenser than it was ten minutes ago, and I couldn't figure out why. The normal atmosphere we had was non-existent. Instead of two close friends having dinner together, it almost felt like two strangers. I wanted to ask if there was something else he wasn't telling me, but if he didn't want to talk about it, I wasn't going to pull it out of him.

So, I just stayed quiet.

***

Rex was in the kitchen when I got home. It was clear he'd been pacing just before I walked inside. His arms were across his chest and he was wearing the same thing as earlier. "How'd it go?" He blurted it out with wide eyes.

"How'd what go?" I took off my jacket and dogged him.

"Dinner. Did Zeke say anything?"

"Of course he did," I snapped. "You think we just sat there quietly all night?" My brother was being weirder than normal right now.

"Well, what did you guys talk about?"

"Stuff." Like none of your business.

"What stuff?" he asked. "Work? The bowling alley? Having feelings for each other?"

"What?" Both of my eyebrows rose. "What did you just say?"

"Running into each other," he corrected. "What did you think I said?"

This conversation was giving me a headache. "I'm just going to change, and I'll be on my way."

"Where are you going?"

I threw my clutch at him. "Stop being nosy."

"Well, I'm leaving too." He headed to the door.

"Wait, where are you going?" I turned around and faced him.

"Stop being nosy." He gave me the bird and walked out.

***

234

I took the elevator to Ryker's floor. The hum of the machine vibrated in my ears. The floors changed as I ascended. I told him I would come by after dinner with Zeke so he was expecting me.

The elevator came to a slow stop before the doors opened.

Ryker stood there in his gray sweatpants. They hung low on his hips, and his washboard abs looked powerful. His arms hung by his sides. He didn't seem intimidating at all—with the exception of his eyes.

He stared at me so hard it looked like he was trying to burn me.

I didn't step out of the elevator because I couldn't think. My eyes were trained on him, and I thought about the last conversation we had. It was filthy—to say the least.

Before the elevator doors closed, I stepped onto the landing of his apartment. He looked down at me, watching every move I made. Then he came to me, both of his hands immediately digging into my hair like he'd been thinking about it all day. He brushed his lips past mine in a teasing way. "I missed you."

"I missed you." My eyes were lidded, and the passion was guiding me forward.

"Ready for our second date?" He hooked his arm around my ass then lifted me against him without exerting any effort.

My legs immediately wrapped around his waist, and my arms hooked around his neck. "It better be romantic."

"You'll definitely get romance, sweetheart." He carried me into the hallway.

"And there better be a meal."

"I'll order a pizza later."

"And there better be some deep conversations."

"I'll talk dirty to you." He entered his bedroom and laid me on the bed. He slipped off my shoes before he moved to my jeans. He unbuttoned them and slowly pulled them down my legs.

I held myself up by the back of my elbows, watching the look in his eyes as he undressed me.

He looked me in the eye as he grabbed the edge of his sweatpants and pulled them off. He didn't have any boxers underneath. It was all him. And he was definitely happy to see me.

I whistled in a flirtatious way.

The same intensity was in his eyes but he smiled faintly. He leaned over me then pressed his face close to mine.

The second we were in contact, my heart sped up. He set my body on fire, and I burned from the inside out.

He gave me a gentle and slow kiss, feeling my lips purposely. It was timeless and didn't seem to go anywhere, but it was pleasurable. My thighs tightened automatically, and my mind drifted in a state between dream and reality.

He kissed my neck before he grabbed the back of my shirt and slowly pulled it over my head. My hair went with it, but then returned to cascading around my shoulders. Ryker watched it fall before he began kissing the hollow of my throat. Quicker than I could process, he unclasped my bra and pulled it down my arms.

His lips moved to my chest, and he kissed the area, devouring me. Each nipple made it into his mouth then he licked the valley between my breasts. "I can't decide what I like more. These tits. Your pretty mouth. Or that sweet pussy." He wrapped his arm around my waist and guided me up the bed until my head rested on a pillow.

I ran my fingers through his hair and looked into his eyes. "Can't it be a tie?"

"I suppose." He kissed me, sucking my bottom lip before he opened his nightstand.

I grabbed his shoulders and moved him to his back, the condom in his hand. "Wait."

He dropped the condom on the bed then moved his palm underneath his head. His fingers moved through my hair, tucking the strands behind my ear. "Just don't make me wait too long."

I moved on top of him and kissed his body the way he kissed mine. My lips tasted his large shoulders, feeling the hot skin burn my mouth. I licked the skin, tasting it.

I traveled down to his chest and explored his body. I wanted to feel every inch of him, to know him in such a profound way that I could remember this moment twenty years from now.

Ryker was quiet but his breathing increased. His hand moved down my back, and he watched everything I did.

I moved to his stomach and kissed the area, feeling his muscles underneath the skin. I kept traveling down, following his happy trail with my mouth. Then I moved to his cock where it lay on his stomach.

He breathed harder when I got there. Instead of just feeling my hair, he fisted it violently.

I started at his balls, licking the sensitive area.

He hadn't been expecting that because he released an involuntary moan.

I sucked the skin into my mouth, making sure my tongue got every inch of it. Then I moved up the base, giving his dick a long stroke of my tongue.

He watched everything I did, his eyes dark.

I kissed the tip and felt the grooves of his head with my tongue. I took my time there since it was the most sensitive part. Once I lavished it with my kisses, I slowly moved down his length, taking all of it into my mouth.

He moaned loudly and yanked on my hair.

I moved up and down his length, going as slow as possible. I didn't want him to come. I just wanted him to enjoy it, to see me worship his cock with my mouth. He always did so many amazing things with his mouth, and I wanted to do the same for him.

When I was finished, I pulled his length out of my mouth and slowly crawled up his body.

He stared at me with bright eyes. "So?"

"The chili dog was better."

He smiled despite the intensity in his eyes. "You're one of a kind, sweetheart."

I pressed my lips against his and gave him a slow kiss, my eyes open. His were too, and he stared at me without blinking.

He grabbed the foil packet and ripped it open before he meticulously rolled it on his base. Then he moved himself against the headboard, sitting up. "I want you on top, sweetheart."

I straddled his hips and gripped his shoulders. "Someone's lazy..."

"I want to see those tits shake in my face." He pointed his dick at my entrance then pulled my hips down, slowly inserting himself until he was completely inside.

"Oh god..." How did I forget how good he felt?

"So tight." His hands gripped my hips, and he guided me up and down.

The fullness was just right. I was stretched to the breaking point. It was a little painful, but that made it feel even better. "Ryker..."

"Mmm...I like it when you do that." He thrust his hips from below.

Together, we moved. I used his shoulders as an anchor to lift myself up and down. He worked me from below, and the product of both was the most amazing sex. He looked me in the eye, watching my every reaction to him. His face darkened in lust, and the sweat marked his chest.

I didn't know if it was my powerful attraction to him, or the fact his dick was a formidable size, but

I was about to come—hard. With Ryker, I was always ready to blow in a matter of seconds. "I'm gonna come..." My behavior was uncontrollable during sex because I couldn't think clearly. My mind was somewhere else, and my carnal aspects were in charge.

He grabbed the back of my neck and gave me a kiss with his tongue. He swirled it with mine in my mouth, and that was like lit dynamite. My entire core tightened, and a wave of heat washed over me.

"Come on my dick."

I wrapped my arms around his neck and rested my head against his as I felt the explosion. I rode him harder because I wanted everything he could give me. My moans turned to screams, and my entire body ripped it half because it felt so damn good.

Ryker watched me, a quiet moan escaping his lips. "So beautiful." He kissed the corner of my mouth before he moved harder underneath me, giving it to me as fast as he could. When he reached his threshold, he tensed underneath me and dug his fingers into the skin of my hips. A moan escaped from his throat, and he buried his face in my chest, squeezing me tightly as he depleted himself.

I rested my head on his, still catching my breath.

Ryker didn't move for nearly a minute. He recovered from the pleasure we both felt before he gave any sign of life. His cock softened and became semi-hard. He gently pulled himself out of me and I moved from his lap. Now that the fun was over, I was exhausted.

Ryker disposed of the condom and cleaned up before he came back to bed.

I knew I should go home, but I was tired. It took me almost a full minute before I found the strength to get up and gather my clothes.

"What are you doing?"

"Going home." I pulled my panties on before I grabbed my bra.

He gave an irritated look. "Am I a pit stop now?"

"No. I just didn't want to be presumptuous."

"Well, you should start." He grabbed my hand and yanked me back to bed. "And get rid of these." He yanked my underwear off my legs and tossed them on the floor.

"This is a sleepover?"

"Yeah. We'll have pizza, a pillow fight in our underwear, and we'll talk."

"That sounds pretty fun."

"What can I say?" he said. "I'm a pretty fun guy." He kissed my shoulder before he pulled me to his chest and hooked his arm around my waist.

"I have to say, this is the best second date I've ever been on."

He chuckled into my ear. "Me too."

Ray of Light

Chapter Eleven

Rex

"Open the door. It's me."

Footsteps were heard on the other side as Zeke came to the entryway. Then he answered my knocks with an irritated look on his face. "I didn't tell her."

I walked inside without being invited. "Dude, I'm so sorry."

"It's not your fault, man." He shut the door and locked it. Automatically, he went to the fridge and grabbed two beers. He tossed one at me before he took a seat on the couch in his living room. His house was close to the bay. The neighborhood was quiet and peaceful.

I felt like shit for Zeke. "I didn't know until you picked her up. She literally told me two seconds before that."

"It's really not a big deal," he said. "You would have told me sooner if you knew."

I felt the bottle in my hands but didn't take a drink. I wasn't sure how to comfort my best friend in the world. "Are you okay?"

He stared at his beer. "Yeah. I just...feel stupid for not doing something sooner, you know? I waited too long, and someone else snatched her up. I have no one else to blame but myself."

"They won't last forever," I said. "You know how Ryker is. This whole thing will be over in a few months, tops."

"Yeah...probably."

"Then you can talk to her about it."

"Maybe."

I still felt bad for him. "You know, you kind of dodged a bullet, if you ask me. I know you like Rae and everything, but she's pretty annoying."

He chuckled then took a drink. "Thanks for trying to make me feel better, but that tactic isn't going to work. She's not the least bit annoying."

"Ha. You don't live with her."

"When she talked about Ryker, she said he was different with her."

"She said the same thing to me."

He peeled the label off the glass. "And she said she was really into him. I've never heard her say that about a guy before..."

Come to think of it, I hadn't either.

"I don't know...this might be more serious than we thought."

"But that isn't Ryker."

"And Rae isn't any normal girl. She's special. He's not stupid. I bet he realizes just how much of a catch she is." Zeke stared at the floor as he spoke. "Maybe this will last a while."

I hoped it didn't. "You never know."

Zeke shook his head. "I've had a long time to tell her how I felt, but I was too much of a pussy. I think I've missed my chance for good."

"Don't say that..."

"I've got to move on. There are other fish in the sea."

"Tons."

"She can't be the only cool girl."

"I meet awesome chicks on a daily basis, man." I patted him on the shoulder. "Or...you could just tell her how you feel anyway. I mean, they've only been seeing each other for a short time."

Zeke didn't even consider it. "I would never do that to her."

"It's not like they love each other."

"Even so...it would be wrong. It'll just mess with her head and make things awkward between Ryker and me."

"Like they aren't already..."

"And if Rae really likes him, I'd be a total dick for messing that up. Maybe Ryker will rise to the challenge and be the man she deserves."

"Maybe..."

"We really haven't given him a chance. I know you and I mess around a lot, and have never been boyfriend material, but if I found the right girl, you know I'd be loyal to her. And I know you would be the same way."

I nodded in agreement.

"So, I'll have to let it go."

"Do you really think you can do that?" Could you get over someone you saw on a daily basis?

"I'm sure I'll stop thinking about her after I sleep around for a while."

"Sex cures all illnesses."

He chuckled. "I hope you're right." He leaned back in the chair and sighed. "So, anything new with you?"

My thing with Kayden came back to mind. "Yeah...something weird happened with Kayden."

"What?"

"Anytime I'm around her, just her and me, she's always weird."

"Weird?" he asked. "I've never noticed."

"Well, it's only when we're alone together. She's quiet and skittish. It's super awkward the entire time. I saw her at the library and tried talking to her, but it was nails down a chalkboard the entire time. So, I asked her to hang out so she would relax around me."

"And how'd that go?"

I still wasn't sure what the hell happened. "Everything was great. We were at a bar having a few drinks. We were laughing and having a good time. That awkwardness was finally gone and everything felt normal. When she went to the bathroom, these two girls gave me their numbers."

"They just walked up to you and handed them over?"

"Yep." Pretty much.

Zeke looked incredulous but he stopped the interrogation. "Then what happened?"

"Kayden came back from the bathroom and then flipped out on me. She said she had somewhere to be and just took off."

"What?" Zeke asked in surprise.

"Yeah, it was a total 180."

"Then what happened?"

"I went after her and chased her down on the sidewalk. When I caught up to her, she was crying.

Crying." I raised both of my arms in surprise. "I have no fucking idea what happened. She told me to leave her alone then took off."

Zeke had a blank look on his face. "None of this is making any sense."

"You're telling me."

"You must be missing something. Did you say something to her?"

"Dude, I was nothing less than polite to her the entire night."

"But maybe you slipped up and said something. Think."

"I really didn't," I argued. "I even paid for her drinks. I was going to take her to dinner even though I'm broke."

"Did the phone numbers bother her?"

I shrugged. "Why would they?"

"Maybe she was pissed you were chasing tail when you should have been paying attention to her."

That didn't add up. "No. Kayden isn't like that. She's not a high-maintenance friend."

Zeke fell quiet as he tried to figure it out.

"Come on, you're a doctor. Use that big-ass brain of yours."

Zeke rolled his eyes and took a drink of his beer. "Maybe she got a bad call when she was in the bathroom. Maybe everything that happened really did have nothing to do with you."

I'd like to believe that. "It was just so sudden. And if something did come up, wouldn't she have told me?"

"Maybe it was personal..."

"Even then, none of us keeps secrets from each other."

"Everyone has skeletons and secrets," Zeke said. "Even if you don't."

"So, you think I should worry about it?"

"Nah," he said. "There's nothing you could have possibly done to elicit that reaction from her. There must be something else going on."

"Yeah."

"So...you said you got two numbers?"

"Why?"

He smiled. "Are you really going to hook up with both of them?"

I chuckled. "You want one?"

"Why not?" he said. "Maybe we can tag-team them if they're down for it."

"Well, they did walk right up to me and ask me out," I said. "There's a good chance they're into kinky stuff."

"Perfect," he said. "Let's set something up."

Chapter Twelve

Rae

My eyes fluttered open and I took in a handsome face. His green eyes burned by their own light, and the hair on his face looked kissable. I remembered everything we did last night and felt my toes curl.

"Do you always sleep like this?"

"Like what?" I asked with a raspy voice.

"For twelve hours straight."

"Well, it's Sunday. I sleep in on the weekends."

"Man, you're lazy." His lips were on me, kissing my neck and shoulder.

"What do you care?"

"My dick cares a lot. I've been patiently waiting for you to wake up so I could get some action."

"You could have started without me…"

"Like that wouldn't have been creepy." He kept kissing me, lavishing me with kisses.

I sat up and pulled the hair out of my face. "I'm hungry."

He pressed his face close to mine, the desperation in his eyes. "It can wait."

"You didn't get me pizza last night like you promised."

"Sorry...I got caught up in other things." He pushed me back down to the bed and moved on top of me.

"Ryker, I have to pee." I put my hand on his chest. "And I need food."

He kept my body pinned to the mattress. "And I need you."

I wrapped my arms around his neck. "Give me what I need, and I'll make it worth your while."

"Hmm..." He stared into my face with a clenched jaw.

"Is this how you treat all your women? Starve them and deprive them of their bodily needs?"

"Just the ones I really like."

I pushed him off then grabbed my clothes.

"What do you need those for?"

"I need to search for food."

"I have a kitchen. I can make you something."

"Cooking is such a pain," I said. "Why don't we go to Waffle Hut? It's right across the street."

"Because we can't be naked."

"Well, we can't be naked all the time."

"Says who?" he challenged.

I pulled my clothes on then fixed my hair. "Well, I'm getting a waffle drowning in a pool of syrup."

He stayed in bed and watched me get ready. Then he finally got up and threw on a pair of jeans and a t-shirt. "You win, sweetheart."

"Actually, my stomach wins. And just a heads-up, it always wins."

***

He sat across from me and drank his black coffee. A plate of egg whites was in front of him.

"That's all you're eating?" I got a combo, which had eggs, bacon, pancakes, and hash browns.

"Yeah." He took a few bites.

"I'm surprised that keeps you full."

"It's pure protein so it's enough."

"Oh." I kept eating, grateful I wasn't eating pure protein. "Do you want a bite?"

"I'm okay," he said. "It's much sexier watching you eat all of that." A twinkle was in his eyes.

"I'll be working this off at the gym tomorrow, so don't judge me."

"Not judgment at all."

I ate every single bite because I was so hungry. When I had dinner with Zeke the night before, I hardly touched it because we were talking so much. By the time the waiter came to retrieve the plates, I was in the middle of a conversation and didn't realize he took my food until it was gone. Basically, I hadn't eaten in twenty-four hours.

Ryker was a slow eater. He switched from sipping coffee to eating a few bites of his meal. He was quiet, staring at me most of the time. "Safari was cool with you staying with me?"

"He's jealous."

"Poor guy."

"I'll make it up to him when I get home. Maybe take him on a walk or something." I finished eating and felt my stomach extend with all the food I shoveled inside it. "Man, I was starving."

"Skipped a few meals?"

"I hadn't eaten anything since lunch yesterday."

His eyes darkened. "I thought you had dinner with Zeke."

"I did but we didn't do much eating."

Now he looked psycho.

I realized how that sounded. "I mean, we were talking a lot, so I didn't get a chance to eat all of my meal."

The smoke cleared. "What were you guys talking about in so much detail?"

"Well, I told him I was seeing you."

"And?"

"And what?"

"What did he say to that?" Ryker abandoned his coffee and food altogether, focusing his attention directly on me.

"Nothing, really." What was he supposed to say? "I told him that it'd been kind of going on for a few weeks, and he didn't seem surprised. He warned me you were a bit of a player, but he also said I could handle myself." The conversation was pretty ordinary.

He nodded slightly, like he was satisfied with that response.

"Zeke and I tell each other everything. I know about all of his lovers, and he knows about mine. It was nice to finally get it off my chest."

"Do you go into detail about it?"

"Usually."

"Hmm..."

"What?"

"I don't have a girl friend like that. I don't tell anyone about my personal life."

"Really?" That sounded terrible. "That's so sad."

"Sad?" he asked. "Why?"

"You don't share your life with someone else? Tell them about the people in your life? How things are going?"

"Well, I have friends," he said. "I just don't tell them what I do in the privacy of my bedroom. Let alone a woman."

"I like it," I said. "I like being that close to someone."

He rested his elbows on the table. "I'm assuming Rex knows?"

"Yeah."

"Did he shit a rainbow?"

"No." I wasn't sure if I should tell him everything Rex said. It might put him off a bit.

Ryker read it in my eyes. "He wasn't happy, huh?"

"Uh...I wouldn't say that."

"He was pissed?"

"No...he just said I should be careful. He likes you as a friend and a person. He says you're loyal and fun to be around. But he said you weren't exactly the kind of guy he wants with his sister. He told me you were bad news and I shouldn't tread into this with ignorance."

"That's not so bad."

"I told them you were different with me." I watched his face for a reaction. I wanted to see the agreement there, to know I was right.

He answered. "I am."

That's all I wanted.

The tab arrived, and Ryker quickly shoved cash inside.

"Let's split it."

"No." He snatched the tab away and placed it on the other side of the table so I couldn't reach it.

"Why?"

"You're my date. I pay for you."

"You think this is a date?" We were at a cheap diner on a Sunday morning. I hadn't showered and my makeup was gone. My hair was all over the place and it refused to be tamed. This was a weird form of the infamous walk of shame.

"Kinda."

I didn't argue because it wouldn't get me anywhere. I quickly learned that Ryker was a bit stubborn. We left the diner then walked outside. Instead of crossing the street to his apartment, I stayed on the pavement.

He stopped and looked at me, unsure what I was doing.

"Well, I should head home. Last night was fun."

His eyes became hooded. He regarded me with obvious confusion. "What makes you think you're going anywhere?"

"Well, it's Sunday. My friends usually come over and we watch football, make lunch, and play board games."

"Every Sunday?" he asked incredulously.

"Pretty much."

He put his hands in his pockets.

"You're welcome to come if you want—"

"I'd love to." He grabbed my hand and pulled me across the street with him. "Just let me shower and we'll go."

"Okay."

We entered his apartment, but Ryker didn't head for the shower. Instead, he grabbed my face and kissed me. He guided me into the bedroom, his entire body consuming mine.

The second he touched me, I melted. I loved those kisses. Now that I was full and had an empty bladder, I was ready to go. My fingers dug into his hair, and I breathed into his mouth, lost in him.

We undressed then moved back to the bed. Ryker positioned me on my hands and knees and came up behind me. He kissed my spine from my ass to the back of my neck. "I've wanted to take you like this since the moment I saw you." He grabbed a fistful of hair and yanked my head back slightly, exposing my mouth to him. Then he kissed me hard before he grabbed a condom from his drawer and rolled it on.

He entered me quickly, stretching me at the same time. Last time he was gentle, but now he just wanted me. I loved the fullness and the way his chest felt against my back. He kissed my shoulder as he moved inside me. Then he pressed his face against my cheek, breathing hard. Like two wild animals, we moved together and gave in to the carnal passion of desire.

"Beautiful." He hooked one arm across my chest and gripped my shoulder, holding on to me as he rocked into me. "Look at me."

I looked over my shoulder and watched him slam into me with everything he had. He stopped thrusting for a moment and gave me a slow kiss that belied the intensity of the rendezvous. It was soft and full of affection. His tongue moved with mine, giving me intimacy on a new level. He brushed his nose against mine before he pulled away and returned his motion in full force.

***

Before I reached for the doorknob of my apartment, Ryker pushed me into the wall and pinned me there. Our fingers interlocked as they dug into the wall. He looked down at me, his eyes focused on my lips. "I better sneak in a few."

"Sounds like a good idea."

He gave me a half smile before he leaned in and kissed me gently. His lips were always addictive, like the best cocaine the world had ever seen. It wasn't just his mouth but the way he used it. He kissed me like he'd fallen hard and deeply in love. I gave in to that fantasy every chance I got.

He pulled away reluctantly when ten minutes had come and gone. "Maybe that wasn't the best idea." He pressed against me, showing off his hard dick through his jeans.

"I can help you get rid of it."

He gave me that same look I always got. The fire burned in his eyes and he became an otherworldly creature—desperate for one thing.

"I can just turn around..." I turned and gave him my ass. "And you can give it to me just like that." I looked at him over my shoulder, biting my bottom lip.

He took a painful breath, his shoulders tensing.

I wasn't being serious, but it was fun to tease him. The longer I watched his face darken, the less of a joke it became. Now I really did want to drop my pants and feel him fuck me right outside the apartment.

He moved closer to me, his face brushing against mine and his hand gliding over my ass. "If you can be quiet."

He called my bluff, but now I didn't think I should call his.

"I think I hear something." Rex's voice came from inside the apartment.

Ryker immediately stepped back and adjusted his jeans.

I straightened up and tried to act natural, like Ryker and I were just talking about the weather or the Space Needle.

Rex opened the door. "What the hell are you doing?"

"Talking," I snapped. "What are you doing?"

"Wondering why quiet voices are coming from outside my apartment."

"Maybe they were ghosts."

Rex actually believed in ghosts, so it was fun to tease him. "Okay, not funny." He stepped away so we could come inside.

I walked inside and felt Ryker grab my hand.

"None of us felt like cooking, so we ordered pizza," Jessie said from her seat at the table.

"She's full of it," Kayden said. "None of us know how to cook."

I rolled my eyes and turned to Ryker. "Would you like a beer?"

"Sure. Whatever you got."

I opened the fridge and handed him a bottle. I grabbed one for myself. It was surprisingly normal considering everyone warned me Ryker was bad news. But it felt like nothing had changed.

Jessie waved me over. "Guess who came in yesterday?"

"Who?" I went to the area between Jessie and Kayden.

"That one cunt I told you about," Jessie said. "She actually tried to make another appointment with me."

"Did you take her?"

"Uh, no." Jessie rolled her eyes. "She didn't appreciate nice hair when she had it. That ship has sailed."

Rex's voice came into my ear. "You fuck with my sister, I will fucking destroy you..."

The second I turned my back, Rex was at it. "Hold on, guys…" I headed into the kitchen and found Ryker cornered by Rex.

"You're my friend and you're a good guy, but my sister is a whole different ballgame. Do not fuck with her. I mean it—"

"Hey, what's going on over here?" I joined them and tried to act casual.

Ryker had the grace to cover for Rex. "We were talking about the game and placing bets."

Rex raised an eyebrow in surprise.

"Oh cool," I said. "Who's your money on?"

"The Steelers," Ryker said. "And I have a feeling Rex is going to lose what little money he has."

"We'll see." Rex walked into the living room and joined Zeke on the couch.

Embarrassed, I sighed. "I'm so sorry—"

"It's fine," he said quickly. "It doesn't bother me. He's just looking out for you. Now that I know what happened when you were young, I totally get it. He means well."

"You're really going to back him up?" Rex just came over here and threatened to destroy him.

"I'd do the same if I had a sister."

It was then I realized I didn't know anything about Ryker. I didn't know where he grew up, if he had any siblings, why he was the way he was...we didn't talk about anything. Actually, all we did was screw. "Even   so..."

"Look, we've gotten past the initial stage of us seeing each other. Now it's smooth sailing from here on out. And I told him this wasn't a hit-it-and-quit-it type of thing. If that were the case, we wouldn't be seeing each other right now. He knows that."

"I'm still mortified..."

He rested his fingers under my chin and lifted my gaze toward him. He looked down into my face, amusement in his eyes. "You think a guy like him could get under my skin?"

"Probably not."

"Nope." He gave me a gentle kiss before he walked into the living room.

My lips felt numb the second his mouth was gone. I turned and looked at my friends. They were both making stupid faces and grinning like idiots.

But then again, I was doing the exact same thing.

***

Safari was by my side the entire afternoon, not wanting to be apart from me anytime soon. He liked

Ryker, even though he was the reason I was gone most of the time.

At the end of the evening, everyone left. They all had work in the morning. There were pizza boxes scattered everywhere, but I didn't feel like cleaning up.

And Rex never cleaned up.

Ryker stayed by my side for the entire evening. Three empty bottles of beer were on the table, his only refuse. "So, can I stay over tonight?"

Since I slept with him last night, I didn't think he wanted to do a back-to-back. "You want to?"

"Why are you always surprised when I say things like that?"

"Because I'm surprised," I said like a smartass.

"You think I want to sleep alone after last night?" he asked. "And this morning?"

"It's just..." I eyed Safari beside me. His head was resting in my lap, and he looked up at me with his puppy dog eyes. "There won't be much room for you."

"Can't Safari sleep on the ground?"

"He can but he won't. Besides, it's his bed."

Ryker seemed more amused than irritated. "How about he sleeps at the foot of the bed?"

"I think I can get him to do that."

"Then that works for me."

"I have to warn you, my bed isn't nearly as nice as yours."

"That's fine," he said. "I care more about the woman in the bed anyway."

"But we both have work tomorrow." Maybe he forgot.

"I can be at the office a little late. You forget, I own the place."

"Just because you own it doesn't mean you can slack off."

"Actually, it does." He smiled in an arrogant way.

"Since I'm sleeping with my boss, do I get special privileges?"

"Actually, yes." He leaned closer to me and lowered his voice. "You can come into my office and give me head whenever you want."

I smacked him playfully in the arm. "I'm never skipping out on work to do that."

"You can give me a lap dance."

"I'm not doing that either."

"I can bend you over on my desk—"

"I'm not doing it."

He gave me a cute pout then kissed the corner of my mouth. "What's the point in screwing the CEO if you don't get anything out of it?"

I didn't want anything out of it. The first time we met, I had no idea who he was, and it didn't matter to me either. I was still drawn to him in an unbreakable away. "You. I get you out of it."

***

"Are you sure you want to do this?" I tried not to laugh. Ryker lay beside me in my queen-size bed, Safari covering both of our bodies with his heavy torso and legs.

Ryker kept moving, trying to get comfortable. "I always like a challenge."

"A challenge to sleep?"

"Just in general." He moved again, trying to snuggle with me. He hooked his arm around my waist but had to slide under Safari's lifeless body. "Damn, he's heavy."

"He loves his treats."

"I'll say..." Ryker finally got comfortable, his head resting on my pillow. He looked into my eyes, a sleepy look on his face. "What made you get a dog? Living in an apartment..."

"He was a stray. He kept walking into the street where the cars were swerving around him. It was only a matter of time before he got hit. So I pulled over and realized he didn't have a tag or a chip. Those mocha eyes were so cute, and I totally fell in love. So, I took him home."

His eyes held a smile. "That was nice of you."

"I used to be a stray until someone took me in." I was lost when Mom passed away. I did a lot of stupid things, hung out with the wrong crowd and started drinking before I was even sixteen years old. I snuck around with bad boys, not the good-hearted sexy ones, and Rex had a lot of shit he had to deal with that never should have been his responsibility. If he hadn't set me straight, I wouldn't have gone to college and gotten my life back on track. I owed my brother a lot.

Ryker's eyes fell in sadness. His fingers brushed my cheek and tucked my hair behind my ear. "You can't be a stray when you're loved by so many people." He kissed the skin just to the right of my nose.

Ryker was much sweeter than I expected him to be. He seemed stiff and serious all the time, but sometimes, that attitude fell and revealed the true man underneath. "You haven't heard from your father?"

My dad ran out on us after I was born. Apparently, he couldn't handle two kids and a depressed partner. "He came back when my mom passed away."

"He did?"

"He tried starting a relationship with Rex and me, but we both wanted nothing to do with him. We were fine on our own. Then Rex threatened to kill him if he kept bothering us. I haven't seen him since."

"Do you think his gesture was sincere?"

"No." Not even a little bit. "I think it was just awkward for him to see us and he didn't know what else to say. He pitied us. I'm pretty sure he has a family somewhere else."

"Why?"

I shrugged. "It's a hunch."

"Well, I don't think you or Rex need him anyway. You've both become exceptional people on your own."

"Thanks."

He kissed my neck then the shell of my ear.

I closed my eyes, my hand resting against his chest. I could feel his heartbeat through the skin. It comforted me, listening to the cadence.

Ray of Light

Ryker shifted his body slightly and sighed. "How do you sleep like this every night?"

I smiled. "You get used to it."

Chapter Thirteen

Rex

I rolled out of my bed and immediately made coffee in the kitchen. I wasn't a big fan of waking up early. If my business ever improved, I'd make sure I didn't have to be there until at least two.

Voices sounded down the hallway as Rae and Ryker headed to the front door with Safari walking behind them.

I told Ryker I'd break both of his legs if he fucked with my sister, and it wasn't an idle threat. She'd spun out of control once before, and I wasn't going to let it happen again. She and I were a team, and if you hurt my comrade, I'd hurt you too. I knew I was far too protective as a brother, but in a really weird and complicated way, I saw her as my own kid.

Ryker said he didn't have any bad intentions toward her, and this wasn't a typical fling like all the others. He told me I should expect to see him a lot more. Apparently, he really liked her.

He better.

I poured a cup of coffee and tried not to stare.

"Sorry last night was so uncomfortable," Rae said with a chuckle.

"It's okay," Ryker said. "I understand I have to share you."

Rae crossed her arms over her chest, awkward that I was nearby. "Well, I'll see you later…"

"Yeah." He cupped the back of her neck and gave her a kiss.

Rae visibly melted the second he touched her. She gripped his biceps like she didn't want him to leave at all.

Dammit. This was serious.

He brushed his nose against hers before he opened the door. "Bye, Safari."

He barked.

Ryker chuckled then waved to me as he walked out. "See you later, Rex."

"Bye, shithead." I kept drinking my coffee.

He laughed at my comment and kept walking. "See ya, lameass."

Rae shut the door behind him then gave me the stink-eye.

"What?" I asked innocently.

"Why are you calling him shithead?"

"I was joking." I poured a bowl of cereal. "That's what guys do."

"No, you weren't joking. You really need to let this go."

"Well, do you need to make out right in front of me?"

"It's my apartment, Rex. Why don't you go somewhere else?" Safari came by her side, following her everywhere she went. "You could have taken your coffee in the living room."

"That's not where I have breakfast."

She rolled her eyes. "Whatever. Be a child about this."

"I will, thank you very much." I sat down and went to town on my Lucky Charms.

She toasted a bagel and smeared cream cheese over it before she sat across from me. "I really hope this bowling alley gets off the ground...and you can move out."

"Me too."

"Zeke was smart for not taking you in."

"He just wants his privacy for all the nasty shit he does."

"No, he just hates you, Rex."

I finished my bowl then poured another. "He loves me."

"When he needs a wingman, maybe."

Safari hopped on the other chair and sat at the table like a person. He was unusually smart and well behaved. I wasn't sure how my sister trained him so well.

She took a few bites of her bagel. "I don't want to go to work today…"

"Can't you use a sick day?"

"Yeah, but I try to avoid it. I just have more work to do when I get back in the lab. It's not worth it."

I didn't understand all the scientific things she did, and I didn't bother trying to understand them. "There's something I want to talk to you about."

"If it has anything to do with Ryker, I'm going to scream." She gave me the most venomous glare of all time. "I'm sick of talking about him."

"Actually, I was going to talk about something else. But while we're on that subject, I don't think you truly understand what you're dealing with. Ryker and I have both fucked the same girl at the same time in the locker room at school. He had her in the front, and I had her in the back. He's had threesomes at least ten times. He even—"

"Rex, I don't care about his past. It has nothing to do with me."

"Uh, you should care a little bit. You really want to spend time with a guy like that?"

"Would you characterize yourself in the same way?"

Huh? I didn't understand the question. "What?"

"Are you two similar? Would you say you guys are the same person?"

"Uh...I guess."

"Well, I think you're a great person, Rex. What you do in your private life is none of my business, and I really don't want to know about it, but I see the other side of you. You're loyal, selfless, compassionate, and so many other things. When you meet the right girl, I know you'll be Prince Charming. Is it really fair to not give Ryker the same belief?"

I spun my spoon in my bowl. "I guess not..."

"Then let it go."

"But what if you aren't the right girl?"

"Whether I am or not, I'm enjoying our time together for now. If it doesn't work out, oh well. Life goes on."

"Really?" I asked. She would have a level head with it?

"Yes." She took a few sips of her coffee. "Now, what were you going to say before we started talking about Ryker...again?"

I got distracted by Ryker and forgot. "I had a weird thing happen with Kayden."

"A weird thing?" Both of her eyebrows rose. "What does that mean?"

I told her the whole story, from beginning to end. "I still don't have a clue what the hell happened. Even Zeke couldn't figure it out. When she was over here yesterday, she ignored me and pretended nothing happened. Please tell me you know something I don't."

She held the mug on the table, and the steam evaporated into the air. Her lips were pressed tightly together as she considered the possibilities. "I really don't know...maybe something happened with her family and she didn't want to tell you about it."

"But wouldn't she tell you?"

"Not necessarily," she said. "We tell each other a lot of things, but our entire lives aren't on display."

"Well, do you think you could talk to her for me? Figure it out?"

"Yeah, I'll bring it up," she said. "But I have a feeling it had nothing to do with you. Your story doesn't suggest it, unless you're leaving something out."

"I told you the whole thing, from beginning to end."

"Then I'd relax. For all we know, she lost her job or something."

"How do you get fired from a library?" It wasn't possible. They were practically volunteers anyway.

"I'm just saying." She finished her coffee then left it on the table. "Well, I've got to get ready. I'll see you after work."

"When are the contractors starting?" I asked as she walked away.

"Not sure. I'll give them a call later."

***

Just when my shift was finally over, Rae and Zeke walked inside. They were talking and smiling like everything was normal. Maybe Zeke was taking this Ryker thing better than I gave him credit for. I was worried he would ignore her for a few weeks until he got over it.

"What's up?" I hopped over the counter.

"So, we've got everything we need," Zeke said. "Everything is officially underway."

"You'll have to close down the place for a few weeks, probably a month," Rae said.

"What?" I blurted. "I can't close. I won't make any money."

"Dude, you aren't making any money now," Zeke said.

"Hey." I pointed at him. "That hurt."

"I'm just saying," Zeke said. "Besides, if you don't have to pay employees or keep the lights on, all you need to worry about is the rent and insurance for the month. So, it's not a big deal."

"I guess it'll be nice to sleep in…"

"And be home 24/7 so I have to see your ugly face constantly," Rae said.

"Maybe you should get a second job," I teased.

Zeke knew a fight was about to begin. "Anyway…they are going to start redoing the lanes, put in the bar, and repainting the walls. The weather forecast says it's going to be sunny this week, so we're going to take advantage of that and add a coat of paint to the outside."

Damn, this place was going to be turned upside down.

"But it's going to look awesome when they're done," Rae said. "And we'll take that time to figure out our strategy. We should definitely make some crazy sales to get people to come in. You probably won't break even at first, but it'll bring more customers in later. And I have another idea. Since Ryker is the biggest news around here right now,

I'm going to ask him to do some kind of bowling challenge for charity. Every reporter and newscaster will be here to record it."

"And boom," Zeke said. "You've got yourself a hopping business."

"Ryker would do that?"

"Of course he would," Rae said. "And not just for me."

I was touched, and I didn't know how to put that into words. They didn't get anything out of this, other than possibly losing their investments, and they still wanted to help me out. "Thanks, guys…"

"No problem." Zeke clapped my shoulder. "We're family, right?"

We were giving the word a whole new definition. "Yeah. We're family."

***

We sat in the bar and downed our beers. A plate of fries was on the table but Rae ate most of them. Zeke acted like nothing had changed and he wasn't just about to tell her they should be together.

It was like it never happened.

"How was work?" he asked Rae.

"Good. Sometimes I get lonely being in there all by myself, but I'm also glad I don't have to deal with people all the time."

"I'd prefer more peace and quiet," Zeke said. "But I don't have that luxury."

"Any interesting patients?"

"I had a woman come in because she said her tits were ugly."

I stopped drinking my beer.

"What?" Rae asked, just as confused as I was.

"She said the skin on her breasts was ugly." He shrugged. "It didn't make any sense when she told me, and it definitely won't make any sense when I tell you. I recommended her to a plastic surgeon because there was nothing I could do for her."

"Were her tits ugly?" I asked.

"Eh." Zeke shrugged. "They were alright."

"But not ugly enough for medical intervention?" Rae asked.

"No, not really," Zeke said. "People have ugly tits all the time. There's really nothing you can do about that unless you involve plastic surgery." Zeke finished his beer then moved on to the next one.

"I hope I don't have ugly tits," Rae said.

"You don't," Zeke blurted automatically. "I mean, from what I can tell."

Rae smiled and didn't seem offended at all. "The way they look through a shirt isn't the same thing."

"I've seen you in a bikini," Zeke said. "Believe me, they're good."

I didn't participate in their conversation because my sister's breasts didn't interest me.

"What kind of weird tits have you seen?" Zeke rested his elbows on the table and looked at me.

"Hmm..." I'd seen a lot of titties in my day. "The cucumber kind."

"The cucumber kind?" Rae asked.

"You know." Zeke demonstrated how they would appear with his hands. "The kind that sorta hang and are skinny, especially when they lean over."

"Yeah," I said. "Those are the worst."

"I didn't realize that was a thing," Rae said. "I just assumed guys didn't like small tits."

"Small boobs are fine," Zeke said. "I like them as much as big ones, as long as they are proportional."

"Yeah, small ones are great," I said. "Honestly, I'm an ass man—through and through."

"That makes two of us." Zeke clanked his beer against mine.

"I'm a sucker for a guy's jawline. You know, the rugged and handsome kind." Rae's voice became more high-pitched, sounding more feminine.

It was ironic because Zeke had the exact jawline she was describing. Now that I thought about it, Zeke was always popular with the girls. They all liked him, and the fact he was a doctor made him even more of a catch. Rae was never into him? Not once?

"Like Clint Eastwood?" Zeke asked.

"Yes, exactly," Rae said.

Zeke rubbed his chin, like he knew he fit the bill. "What else?"

"I like them tall," Rae said. "I guess because I'm a little tall for a woman."

"No, you're perfect," Zeke said automatically.

Rae was totally oblivious to the true meaning of his compliments. Now that I knew how Zeke felt, I realized just how obvious it was. The only way he could top it was if he held a sign that said, "I love you."

"So, how's it going with Ryker?" Zeke asked the question hesitantly, like he was only asking to act normal.

"Good," she said. "He stayed over the other night. He's not a big fan of Safari."

"Well, he better start," Zeke said. "That's Safari's home."

"I don't think the problem is with him, just the fact that he covers the entire bed when we sleep." Rae chuckled before she took another drink.

"That's Safari's bed," Rex said. "Where else is he gonna sleep?"

"I doubt Ryker will be staying over anymore," Rae said. "A big dog and a big man just don't mix together."

I'd come to the realization I needed to drop my prejudice against Ryker. My sister had already made up her mind about him, so I should just accept it. If she got hurt, she couldn't say I didn't warn her. Sometimes I forgot that she was an intelligent adult. She was the one taking care of me at that very moment. She was paying all my bills and even giving me an allowance. A woman like that could clearly take care of herself.

"Seeing anyone?" Rae asked.

"Not seriously," Zeke said. "I hooked up with this girl last night."

He left out the fact that I was there, with my own chick.

"How'd that go?" Rae asked.

"The sex was good. But I won't call her again."

She was definitely a hit-it-and-quit-it kind of girl, not one you brought home to your parents.

"Why not?" Rae asked.

Zeke shrugged. "I'm not that interested."

Zeke didn't have relationships very often. He played the field most of the time, just the way I did. Personally, I'd never had a girlfriend—ever. I loved my freedom way too much.

"You must have your pick of the crop," Rae said. "A handsome doctor…"

Zeke shrugged.

"Just make sure you only settle for someone who's amazing," Rae said. "Because you're amazing."

His eyes softened.

"Did you ever talk to Kayden?" I asked.

"No," Rae said. "I haven't had a chance."

"What do you mean?" I snapped. "Just call her."

"I can't corner her like that. It's rude." Rae was a lot more sensitive to people than I was.

"Well, I need to know."

"I'll ask her to lunch tomorrow," Rae said. "And I'll tell you what I find out. But I'm sure it had nothing to do with you."

I really hope so.

Rae could tell I was still concerned. "You're worrying over nothing, Rex."

"I think so too," Zeke said. "If she had a problem with you, she wouldn't have come over on Sunday."

I guess that was true.

***

Now that I wasn't working, I was bored out of my mind. I didn't like going to work and spraying the inside of smelly shoes with Febreze and Lysol, but sitting at home all day was somehow worse.

I watched everything on daytime television, played a few games, called up a regular to screw, and then I went back to watching TV. Safari kept me company but he just laid on me the entire time.

Rae came in the apartment shortly after five.

"I never thought I'd be so happy to see you." I actually pulled her in for a hug. "Let's do something. Anything. How about we hit the courts and play some ball?"

"Someone needs to get some friends..."

"I do have friends but they're all at work."

"Well, I'm going to Ryker's for dinner."

It was a testament to how bored I was when I spoke again. "Can I tag along?"

"To dinner with us?" she asked incredulously. "Uh, no."

"Please," I said. "I'm so bored I'm losing my mind."

"Find something to do."

"Dude, I've done everything. I watched TV, played video games—"

"Cleaned the house?" She looked around at the dirty dishes in the sink, the spaghetti stain on the tile, and the bag of popcorn sitting out on the counter.

"Well...that's a last resort."

"I'm not blowing off my date if you won't even clean up after yourself."

"Okay, okay." I was really desperate. "I'll clean the whole house if you let me come along."

She crossed her arms over her chest and looked at me in a whole new way. "Damn, you're really, really bored."

"That's what I've been trying to tell you."

"I guess I can cancel on him. It shouldn't be a big deal."

I grinned from ear-to-ear.

"Besides, it'll just make him want me more." Her eyes were full of confidence, and her lips rested in the form of a light smile. "What do you want to do?"

"Let's go to the arcade."

"That sounds like fun."

"Awesome." My sister annoyed me like crazy, but she always came through for me.

She grabbed her phone and called Ryker. "Hey, I was wondering if we could reschedule. Can we go out tomorrow night?"

Ryker's voice could be heard through the phone. "Why? Is everything alright?"

"Everything is fine. Rex is just bored from not working, and he wants me to spend time with him."

Ryker didn't hold back his disappointment. "Why am I the one who has to suffer for him being a loser?"

"I can hear you, jackass," I said loudly.

"Good," Ryker snapped. "I was hoping you could."

Rae rolled her eyes. "Tomorrow?"

Ryker sighed into the phone. "Why don't you just bring him with you?"

"Because that wouldn't be fun for either of us."

"I don't care," he said. "I just want to see you."

I couldn't keep my surprise back at that comment. Who knew Ryker was affectionate.

"Tomorrow," she pressed.

"I'll make a compromise with you," Ryker said. "You can go out with him, but you sleep here with me."

I made a gagging face.

"You have yourself a deal," Rae said.

"Good," he said. "I expect you here by nine. What are you guys doing anyway?"

"We're going to go to the arcade." Rae waited on the line for him to say something.

He was quiet for a long time. "The arcade?" The sound of longing was unmistakable. "Like, the big one downtown?"

"Yes." Rae smiled because she knew where this was going.

"Well...can I come along?" he asked hopefully.

"You guys are both five-year-olds," Rae said with a sigh.

"The arcade is awesome," Ryker said. "I'll never grow out of that place."

Rae turned to me. "Is it cool if Ryker comes?"

I couldn't say no even if I wanted to. I interrupted their plans to begin with. "Sure."

Rae turned back to the receiver. "Can you be here in an hour?"

"Sweetheart, I'll be there whenever you want me to be."

I shoved my finger down my throat and pretended to gag.

Rae kicked me in the shin. "See you then."

***

"Dude, *Ms. Pac-Man* is the best game ever." I used to play it all the time as a kid. Even when there was no one else to play with, it was a great game.

"Definitely a classic," Ryker said.

"I'm gonna get a soda. My hand is cramping." Rae was great at video games, probably because she played them with me all the time.

Ryker watched her go before he turned back to me. "Want to have a match?"

"Depends," I said. "Are you ready to be castrated?"

"Your sister already did that when she beat me at *Mortal Kombat*."

I put the quarters in the machine and we started to play. We both had our own screens and got all the white dots and the fruit extras. Ryker was just as good as I was, and soon it became tense.

We kept playing until one of us lost our three lives first. Thankfully, it was Ryker.

"Sucker," I said.

"You just got lucky." He glanced over my shoulder and looked at Rae, constantly keeping her in his sights.

It would take me a while to get used to the fact that they were together.

"Can I ask you something?"

"I guess," I said. "You just did."

"Is Zeke going to be a problem?"

I froze on the spot and forgot to breathe. "Huh?"

"I know Zeke is into her. Is he still after her?"

How did he know that? He said it with such certainty I couldn't believe it. There was no way Zeke would tell him. Did Rae know how Zeke felt and tell Ryker? That didn't seem likely either. "I don't know where you're getting that from, but it's not true." I'd cover for my best friend until the end of time.

"It's obvious in the way he looks at her." He said it with complete confidence, like there was no room for misinterpretation.

"Well...I guess that's your opinion."

Ryker ignored what I said. "Will he be a problem for me?"

"Zeke isn't the type of guy to interfere in a relationship, if that's what you're worried about.

Just the other day, he and I tag teamed these two chicks. He's the last person you should be worried about."

He nodded in satisfaction. "I'm glad to hear it."

I stuck my hand in my pocket and looked for more quarters.

"You seem a lot more relaxed about Rae and me." Ryker was different than Zeke and I. He alluded to things rather than just coming out and saying them.

"I knew I needed to back off."

"I really hope you and I can be the friends we were before." He crossed his arms over his chest. "Because your friendship does mean something to me."

"Just don't fuck with my sister and nothing will change."

"That seems pretty simple."

When I looked over my shoulder, Rae was eating a corn dog while seated at the table.

Ryker grinned from ear-to-ear. "She can make anything look sexy."

I cringed. "Keep it PG around me. Otherwise, I'll throw up all over your shoes."

"I'll try." Instead of walking over to Rae, he stood by me. There was no other explanation for it unless he had something else to say. "Rae told me about your mom... I'm sorry."

I assumed he already knew. "Thanks."

"She told me you took over as her legal guardian. That must have been rough."

"It wasn't a walk in the park..." That was an understatement. It was damn hard. Rae was difficult to manage because she went into shock. She started doing crazy things, and I had to go from being a knucklehead to a dad overnight.

"I want you to know I would never hurt Rae on purpose. I care about her and will always respect her the way she deserves. I can't promise we'll be together forever or anything like that, but I won't cause her any further pain. She's an incredible woman, and I'm not oblivious to that."

Those words finally put me at ease. The last time we spoke about this, I got in his face and threatened to kill him. He never had a chance to say anything because Rae came over. The fact that he said all of that with such sincerity made me realize he wasn't taking her for a ride like all the others. It didn't seem like he loved her, but it seemed like he really did care for her. And that's all I could ask for. "You're a good guy, Ryker."

He smiled then clapped me on the shoulder. "You're a good brother, Rex."

I cleared my throat. "Should we go over there and stop her from eating everything at the concession stand?"

He chuckled. "I think that's a good idea."

Ryker and I joined Rae at the table. The paper tray was empty with the exception of the ketchup and mustard. She sipped her soda then handed it to Ryker. He took a long drink, holding eye contact with her.

I tried to ignore it.

"Hungry?" Ryker asked.

"I couldn't turn down a corn dog," Rae said. "I love those things."

He sat beside her. "I know you do, sweetheart."

I tried to ignore that too. "We need more quarters."

"I don't have any more cash," Rae said.

"What good are you?" I demanded.

"I just gave you twenty bucks to spend at the arcade," Rae argued. "That's generous enough."

Ryker put his arm around her waist, being more affectionate with her than usual. It was probably because he knew I was finally cool with everything.

"By the way, I spoke to Kayden today," Rae said casually.

"What did she say?" I blurted.

"She said she got a message that her grandmother was sick." Rae gave me a triumphant look. "I told you it had nothing to do with you."

I breathed a sigh of relief. "Oh, thank god. I thought I really did something stupid."

Ryker furrowed his eyebrows. "What are you guys talking about?"

I told him the story for what felt like the zillionth time. "At least it had nothing to do with me. I'd kill myself if I made her cry."

Ryker had the same look on his face, like he was still confused. "If that's true, why did she come back from the bathroom and talk with you for a little bit? Why did she get upset after you showed her the phone numbers?"

I shrugged. "I don't know. Maybe something triggered it."

He didn't seem convinced. "It sounds like the phone numbers set her off. Maybe she was jealous you were hitting on other women."

"But that doesn't make any sense." At all. Why would she care?

"It does if she has feelings for you," Ryker said with confidence. "Why else would she always be quiet around you but normal around everyone else? Why would she storm out after you said two beautiful women just hit on you? Am I the only person who has connected the dots?"

"That's just not possible," I said. "I've known Kayden for...a hundred years now. She doesn't see me like that."

"Or does she?" Ryker said.

I turned to Rae. "Ryker is off his rocker, right?"

Rae pressed her lips tightly together. "I can't picture Kayden having a thing for my brother. It would have come up a million years ago."

"Maybe it's a recent development," Ryker said.

"I find that unlikely," Rae said. "She would have told me. And if she didn't, she would have told Jessie, who would have told me."

"When's the last time she had a boyfriend?" Ryker asked.

I shrugged because I had no idea.

Rae searched her mind. "I'm not sure... It's been a while."

Ryker had a triumphant look on his face. "I'm telling you, that's it."

I still wasn't convinced. "Nah. I'd believe that grandmother story over that any day."

"Me too," Rae said.

"Whatever," Ryker said. "I guess time will tell."

Kayden didn't see me as anything other than a friend. If she did, she would have hit on me or something. She was beautiful with a smoking body. She could have anyone she wanted. There was no reason why she wouldn't just walk up to me and tell me she wanted to jump my bones if that's how she felt.

I knew I was right.

Chapter Fourteen

Rae

I moved out of his arms before he could snatch me again. "I shouldn't stay. I've got work tomorrow."

Ryker continued to lie on the bed, looking gloriously naked. His chest was like a slab of concrete. I loved digging my nails into the muscle when I rode him like a stallion. His semi-hard dick lay on his stomach, and his muscular thighs and toned legs stretched out before him. "What does that matter?"

"I'd have to get up early and go home. You know me. I treasure my sleep."

"You could just bring your stuff here..." He rested his hands behind his head.

"Too much preparation." I found my panties and pulled them on.

He sat up and leaned back on his elbows. "Give me a kiss before you go."

I stared at him suspiciously, wondering if it was some kind of ploy. He always walked me to the door so why would he want a kiss now? "That's an odd thing to say..."

"That I want a kiss?" he asked. "I don't think so. I love kissing your lips—both of them." He kept the same look on his face, one of innocence.

Something was off. I could feel it.

"Fine." He lay down again. "But don't expect me to kiss you when you're in the mood for it."

Finally convinced there wasn't any foul play, I crawled over the bed to plant a kiss on his lips. I inched closer until I was hovering over him.

He looked up at me with a slight smile on his lips. Then he went for it.

He grabbed my arm and twisted me until I was on my back. He moved on top of me, pinning me down with his enormous size. His lips hovered over mine, along with a look of victory in his eyes.

"Damn, I knew you were up to something."

"These lips aren't going anywhere." He gave me a slow kiss before he brushed his nose against mine.

"I have to get up thirty minutes earlier just to get to my apartment before I shower."

"Then don't go to work tomorrow. You'll get a paid leave of absence."

I rolled my eyes. "That doesn't solve anything. I want to work."

"Your priority should be pleasing your boss."

"And your priority is going to run your business into the ground."

He smiled. "There are more important things in life." He settled beside me and pulled me into his chest, locking his arms around me so I couldn't escape. He pressed a few kisses to the back of my neck.

"I need to feed Safari."

"I'm sure Rex, however stupid, can manage."

"And I didn't take him for a walk today."

"You can do it tomorrow."

"I have laundry to do."

He tightened his arms more. "Make all the excuses you want. You aren't going anywhere."

I sighed and felt my body give in to the fatigue. It took all my energy to get out of bed the first time. There was no way I could manage it a second time. "You're the devil."

"And you're an angel." He kissed my bare shoulder and made my skin come alive. "You're the light to my dark."

"I don't know... I'm pretty dark."

"I've yet to see it."

"For one, I'm sleeping with my boss. That's pretty skanky."

"You didn't know I was your boss."

"But I do now. Yet, here I am."

He kissed the back of my neck. "I think it's sexy."

"Actually, your dick thinks that."

"Believe me, we aren't that different. Whatever he's thinking, I'm thinking." He rested his face in the crook of my neck and pressed his hard-on into the area between my cheeks.

"It's almost one in the morning," I whispered. "We should get some sleep."

"Why sleep when I can look at you?" He kissed the shell of my ear.

"You're never satisfied, are you?"

"No, I'm always satisfied." He pressed his lips to my ear. "I just love being satisfied over and over." His fingers played with my underwear until he pulled them to the side. Then he pressed his tip against my entrance, the thick cock stretching me wide.

It felt so good I forgot about getting up early the next day.

He got his head inside and moaned when he realized how wet I was.

Sometimes, I wished I could hide it from him.

"I knew you didn't want to leave." He gripped my hip as he moved farther inside me.

I grabbed his hand and squeezed it when I realized something. "You forgot a condom."

He stopped moving, his dick already halfway inside me. "You're on the pill, aren't you?"

Yes. But I never told him that.

"And we aren't sleeping with anyone but each other." He kissed my ear as he spoke. "No condom." He started to move again, his body tensing in pleasure at feeling me bare.

I grabbed his hip and steadied him. "Whoa, hold on." I wanted to keep going, but my health was more important. "I'm not going to have unsafe sex."

"It is safe."

"How do I know it is? How many girls have you slept with?"

He sighed in irritation.

"We don't have to have the conversation if you just put something on."

He stilled, like he was about to open his drawer and pull a rubber on. "I don't have anything. But if I get checked out, can we go bareback?"

He was willing to get checked out? That sounded like too much work for a guy. "Yes."

"Then I'll do it tomorrow." He pulled out of me then rolled a condom on. When he was ready, he was on me again, grabbing my thigh and lifting it up as he inserted himself inside me.

I gripped the sheet as he stretched me to the limit.

One hand snaked around my neck, and he left it there, keeping me in place as he had me.

I'd never been grabbed like that before, and I actually liked it.

He slammed into me like he owned me, like I was his plaything to do whatever he wanted. He breathed hard into my ear as he thrust at a quick pace.

I gripped his forearm and just enjoyed it.

"Say my name, sweetheart."

"Ryker..."

He twisted my face toward his and looked down at me with fiery eyes. Then he gave me an aggressive kiss to match. "Your pussy is fucking crack."

An involuntary moan escaped my lips, practically coming out as a scream.

"And it's mine."

***

I removed my lab coat and goggles before I washed my hands in the sink. My hands were cracked and dry from washing them so much.

Whenever I wasn't at work, I lathered them in lotion. Otherwise, they would callus.

"Clocking out?" Ryker's voice sounded from behind me.

I couldn't pretend to be surprised. I'd grown used to him popping up whenever my back was turned. "Yep." I dried my hands with the paper towels then retrieved my belongings from my locker.

"Had a good day?"

"It was all right," I said. "I had a hard time focusing because I was so tired." I shot him a glare.

He smiled and didn't show an ounce of remorse. "Maybe you should have taken the day off like I offered."

I shouldered my bag then walked up to him. "Well, I'm going to head home. I'll see you later."

He grabbed me by the wrist so I wouldn't go anywhere. The touch was gentle but hinted at everything he wanted to do to me right on my table. "There's something I want to give you." He pulled out a folded piece of paper and handed it to me.

I opened it. "What is it?"

"Read it."

It was the lab results from his STD panel. It said he was clean. "You thought it was the best idea to give this to me at work?"

"Jenny is gone for the day, right?"

"Not the point." I folded it up and placed it in my purse.

"I'm clean like I told you."

"Good to know."

"So...let's go to my place."

"Right now?" I asked incredulously.

"Yep."

"I'm going to head home. I haven't spent time with Safari, and I'm sure Rex has trashed the house by now."

Ryker gave me a look of murder.

"Maybe you're used to girls doing whatever you say, but I'm not one of those girls."

"I've noticed," he said darkly.

"I'll see you later."

"Like, later today?" he pressed.

"I don't know," I said. "Whenever."

He grabbed me by the wrist again. "Pack your things and stay with me tonight. This is not up for discussion."

I'd always had a hard time taking orders— always. "Excuse me?" Maybe other girls liked being bossed around by a beautiful man, but I didn't. "Ryker, I'll see you whenever I see you. I have other people in my life besides you." I twisted from his grasp just the way Rex taught me.

Ryker knew he crossed a line with me. "I'm sorry. I didn't mean to be so...forceful. I'm not myself."

He seemed sincere so I let it go. "It's okay."

"I just..." Ryker never struggled to get his words out. He was usually eloquent and quick on his feet. "Never mind."

"Maybe I'll see you tomorrow."

Disappointment was on his face, but he didn't make a further argument. "Okay."

I stepped around him to the door.

Ryker grabbed me again. "No kiss goodbye?"

"Not when we're at work." I pulled away and kept walking.

"Then you better make up for it later." His playful smile had returned.

The Ryker I'd fallen for was back. "Ten times over."

***

The second I walked in the door, he was all over me. His hands were in my hair and his lips suffocated mine. His dick was hard like he'd been thinking about me before I even walked inside.

He picked me up and carried me to his bedroom, his lips running down my neck.

I'd never felt sexier with another man. Ryker made me feel special, like I drove him wild with desire. And he did it without the use of words.

The second I was on the bed, he pulled my clothes off, stripping me down until I was naked and ready to go. He only had his sweatpants on, so he kicked those aside and climbed on top of me.

He pressed his face to the area between my legs and did all the things I loved with his tongue. He made me forget about everything else in the world and had me focus on him alone. I lay back and writhed as he pleased me in such a profound way.

When I was just on the verge of release, he stopped and climbed on top of me, separating my thighs with his as he prepared to enter me. His cock was rock-hard and eager.

He sucked my bottom lip and nibbled on it gently before he inserted his tip inside me. My slickness was abundant so he had an easy time squeezing through. Once he was completely inside me, he released the loudest moan I've ever heard. "Fuck."

His cock felt even better without latex. I could feel his hardness with more definition, and the way he slid back and forth was even more tantalizing. My nails ran down his back as he moved.

He rocked into me with long, even strokes. Sometimes he would slow down to kiss me, planting soft caresses to the corner of my mouth. Then he would speed up again, looking me in the eye as he rocked.

Within minutes, my body tensed then released. I screamed and dug my nails into his back, loving the fact that every single orgasm he gave me lasted forever. They were powerful and made my spine ache from the intensity.

Ryker prepared for his moment. He separated my legs farther and gave slow strokes, breathing hard and preparing for the blast. Grunts came from the back of his throat as he moved.

I grabbed his ass and pulled him farther into me. "Come inside me."

That was the trigger to his threshold. He pressed his face to mine as he released, filling me with his warmth. There was a distinct heaviness inside me, and the fact that his seed was so abundant turned me on all over again.

When he was finished, he stayed on top of me, his dick softening inside me. Sweat was on his chest, and I kissed it away. He continued to breathe hard before he slowly pulled out of me. He turned over and lay on his back, his eyes on the ceiling. "Shit, that was good."

"It really was…" Now I was ready to go to sleep.

***

Ryker massaged my scalp with the shampoo, digging into my hair with his large hands. His eyes trailed over the soap suds that drifted down my body. "Did you bring a bag?"

"No."

"Why not?" He kept the aggression out of his voice, but the tone was still there.

"Because I don't plan on sleeping over."

"Why don't you want to sleep here?"

I loved staying with Ryker. Having a hunky man to hold me all night was a dream come true. When I woke up the following morning, my day would start off right with an awesome orgasm. And the kisses he gave me were the best. I'd never been kissed like that in all my life. "I do want to sleep here. Just not every night. The weekends are fine."

"How are they any different than weekdays?"

"Because I have work in the morning. I have other responsibilities with friends and family." Basically, I had a life. Just because I had a boyfriend didn't mean I was going to drop everyone. It was okay if I spent less time with them, but to bring it down to less than a few times a week was horrendous. I'd had friends who ditched me the second Mr. Right came along. I wasn't going to do the same thing.

He sighed in disappointment.

Ryker didn't strike me as the kind of guy who wanted a woman around all the time anyway. He seemed like a loner, wanting to do things on his own. His darkness and intensity suggested it. "Why do you want me here all the time?"

"What kind of question is that?" He grabbed a bar of soap and rubbed it into my skin.

"A simple one."

"I like being with you. I thought that was obvious."

"But all the time?" I asked in surprise.

He shrugged. "I don't get it either. And I'm sorry you don't feel the same way." He didn't make eye contact with me again. He focused on scrubbing my body with the bar.

"It's not that I don't feel the same way, Ryker." I'd already allowed my walls to fall too far. If I let them come down any lower, I was afraid of what would happen. There were a hundred chains wrapped around my heart, and with every passing week, one more came loose. "I just..."

"Just what?" he pressed.

"I don't want to get too deep until I know what this is."

His eyes returned to mine but his expression was unreadable.

Now that the subject had been broached, I wanted him to give me an answer. What was this? We weren't seeing anyone else and we were together, but what did that mean?

Ryker moved the bar to his own arms and lathered the soap everywhere. "I don't have an answer for you. All I know is, I've never done this before."

"Done what, exactly?"

"I've never wanted a girl to stay over before. Sleepovers aren't my thing. I've never given someone my fidelity. That's new too. I've never thought about one person so much before. Usually, I forget their name soon after we're done." He spoke with confidence, not an ounce of shame inside him.

"All of this is new territory for me. I'm just as confused as you are."

His words filled me like a balloon, but the lack of concrete statements also unnerved me. "What is it about me that you're drawn to? When we first met, you moved on and forgot about me when I declined your offer. After we slept together, you still didn't want to see me again. So, what changed after that?"

He lathered shampoo in his hair then rinsed it out. His eyes were lifeless, hiding everything from me. The silence stretched on forever. Water splashed on the tile below our feet, making background noise. "I'm not sure, Rae. All the women I've been with have wanted something more. But you...you were able to walk away without any expectation in the world. The fact that you were so...confident with yourself to carry on caught me by surprise. You didn't wait around for me, and you were even fine with your friend sleeping with me. I guess...that caught my attention. And the fact that you're independent, strong, funny... and so many other things stuck with me. I haven't stopped thinking about you and don't think I can stop thinking about you. You're different than all the others and...I'm not ignorant of that."

Did that mean I was special? That I meant something to him? He wanted to be around me all the time and he always treated me with respect. There was never a time when I felt like he didn't care. "Do you see this going somewhere?"

"That's too advanced for me," he said quickly. "But I won't be going anywhere anytime soon." He ran his fingers through his hair while holding my gaze.

"Why are you the way you are?" It was something I wanted to know for a while. I understood why Rex and Zeke were like that. They simply didn't care enough about anyone so far, but they were open to the idea of a commitment. Ryker was the complete opposite.

"I like being alone." He said it calmly, like it was absolutely normal to say something like that. "I like having my own space. I like getting what I need from someone then moving on with my life. I like...my freedom."

It was the saddest thing I've ever heard. "But why?"

He shook his head. "I guess I've been let down a lot in the past."

"So, you've been in a relationship before?" That made me feel better. Maybe he was with someone, and she broke his heart. That wouldn't make him cold, just scared.

"No. Never."

Oh. "Then who's let you down?"

It was clear he wasn't going to answer me by the look on his face. "It doesn't matter."

Just when I thought he was opening up to me. "How many women have you been with?"

A slight moment of irritation came into his eyes. "Does it matter?"

"I'd like to know but you aren't required to tell me anything, Ryker. Just keep in mind that while I don't know the number, I know it's high. And I already knew you had serious relationship issues, but I'm still here. So, you don't need to hide who you are. I already know."

His eyes softened slightly, like he was remembering who was asking the question rather than the question itself. "I don't know an exact number but probably over three hundred."

That's so many...

"But keep in mind, that's over the course of about ten years."

That didn't matter. The number was still ridiculous. "And they were all flings?"

"Pretty much. One-timers."

"One-timers?"

"One-night stands," he explained. "I don't usually sleep with the same person more than once. Not exciting after the first time."

Then why had he slept with me at least twenty times?

He studied my face. "Do you think less of me?"

"No," I said automatically.

"Are you lying to me?"

"No."

He relaxed again. "I want you to know that's not how I feel about you. I don't know what I can offer you or where this is going, but I can at least tell you that much."

"I know." It didn't feel like a meaningless fling. Whenever we were together, it felt like a lot more, like he was my boyfriend. He kissed me for no reason at all, and he still wanted to be with me even when no sex was involved. I believed this could go somewhere if I gave it a chance. The chains around my heart were becoming brittle and fatigued from the constant strain. They wanted to come loose and give this relationship everything it deserved. Despite his issues, I'd fallen for him. There was nowhere else I'd rather be than with Ryker.

"And for what it's worth, I've never had sex without a condom before. My first time was with you."

"Never?" I asked with a gasp.

He shook his head.

"How is that possible?"

"Because I've never slept with the same person enough times to allow it. So, I knew I was clean before I even took that test."

It wasn't a declaration of love or a marriage proposal, but it was something. Maybe he couldn't promise me forever, but he could at least promise me tomorrow. He showed me how he could be in the beginning of our friendship. When he didn't get what he wanted, he moved on. But he also showed me how much he could change when he wanted to. He set his eyes on me, and he was still here. He wanted to sleep over every night. He wanted me to be his alone. He asked for monogamy because he only wanted to be with me. It was still risky, but every relationship was risky. "I think it does mean something."

***

I let Safari off the leash, and the second he was free, he sprinted into Zeke's backyard and started running in circles. His tongue flopped around as he ran, the excitement burning in his eyes. "What a dork."

Zeke stood beside me, a beer in his hand. "He's just excited to run around."

"I know," I said with a sigh. "One day, I'll get a house so he can sniff everything and pee on the bushes."

Zeke walked back inside and I followed him. "Where's the dipshit?"

"He said he had to do something before he headed over."

"Do what?" Zeke asked.

I shrugged. "He didn't tell me." I sat on his comfy couch and grabbed my beer from the table.

"Maybe we don't want to know." He gave me a knowing look.

"Yeah, you're probably right."

He sat at the opposite end of the couch. "So, what's new with you?"

Ryker was the only thing on my mind. Our last conversation kept playing over and over. I'd come across men who had commitment issues but nothing like this. "Nothing much."

Zeke knew me better than anyone, even Rex. "Something is on your mind. I can tell."

"How?"

He took a long drink of his beer. "Your shoulders are more tense than usual. Your breathing is different. You sigh a lot more than you usually would. You make eye contact less frequently. It seems like your mind is somewhere else in the middle of a conversation. You touch your hair a lot, putting it behind your ears or just playing with it..."

Damn. He knew me better than I thought. "It's about Ryker..."

He looked away. "Trouble in paradise?"

"Uh...I don't know."

He leaned back into the couch and looked up at the ceiling. "I can tell this is going to be complicated."

"It is."

"Lay it on me."

Zeke was probably a good person to talk to because he was hardly ever in a relationship. Rex was more similar to Ryker, but it was too awkward to have that kind of conversation with him. "Everything has been going well. We spend a lot of time together and there haven't been any problems. But he pesters me to stay over all the time. Whenever I want to go home or do something else, he doesn't want me to leave."

"Isn't that a good thing?"

"It is. But then it made me wonder where our relationship was going. I've given our relationship a chance, but I've had my guard up at the same time. While I know he's different with me, I'm not stupid."

"And did you ask him about it?"

"I did."

Zeke turned his gaze on me and watched me for a few seconds. "I'm guessing this is where the trouble comes into play..."

"He said he's never had a relationship before. He's hardly slept with the same girl twice. I'm the first girl he's had this kind of connection with. He's never been monogamous with anyone in his entire life."

"Well...it sounds like things are different with you."

"But he doesn't know if he could ever give me more than what we have now. Which is fine, I guess. But what if..."

"What if what?"

I fall in love with him. "Things become more serious."

Zeke set his beer down and crossed his arms over his chest.

"I don't know if I should get out of this relationship now or stick it out." I turned to him. "What do you think?"

He rubbed the back of his neck as he considered my question. "I'm not going to tell you what you should do. Never take anyone's advice when they aren't in the same situation. But I'll tell you this. If Ryker's never been like this with anyone before, there's a good chance you're really important to him. If he's already changed that much, he'll probably keep changing. He's not stupid. He understands he found a diamond in the rough."

I smiled.

"But, I also think you're in store for a lot of headaches. Ryker is just as confused as you are, and he's going to screw it up somewhere down the line. You're going to get hurt regardless if he's trying to avoid it. Whatever issues he has, they aren't going away overnight. It'll be a long, uphill battle. Rae, you can have whomever you want. It'll save you a lot of time if you just found someone who could give you exactly what you want."

It was definitely more practical. And it made a lot more sense. If I dated a normal guy and knew it was going to go somewhere if the chemistry was right, I'd be much happier. I'd done the fuck buddy thing before. It was fine, a lot of fun, and involved great sex, but I got hurt in the end because he didn't commit just like he warned he wouldn't. Ryker is very similar to that. "But there's a problem with that..."

"What?" Zeke asked.

"I don't want anyone else." I knew it deep in my heart. Whatever I felt for Ryker wasn't superficial or empty. There was a deep connection there, and I could date a hundred guys but never stop thinking about him. "I don't know why I feel this way...but I do."

Zeke bowed his head and sighed, like he was more disappointed by that response than I was. "I know Ryker is suave and charming or whatever. The girls always like him and I understand why. But you could have someone just as amazing if you looked a little harder." He raised his head and looked me in the eye. "You could have a guy who kisses the ground you walk on but doesn't act like a pussy at the same time. You could have a man who will give you everything you could possibly want and not hurt you along the way. He could rock your world every night and make your toes curl. And at the end of the day, he would always make sure you knew how much he loved you." Zeke continued staring into my eyes, like he was trying to tell me something else.

When the stare became too intense, I looked away. "No man has ever swept me off my feet like that. Only Ryker." I remembered the last man I dated. "The last guy I was seeing shoved his tongue up my nose."

"That date never should have happened," he said. "You don't need a blind date anyway."

"I was trying to get out more..." I chuckled because it was one of the worst dates I'd ever had. "At least it's a funny story to tell."

He smiled. "Yeah, I guess it is funny."

"Zeke, have you ever been in love?" If he had, he never told me about it.

"Um..." He turned his gaze away again. "No, I haven't. But I know I could be."

"What does that mean?"

"There was this girl I was really into...but she never noticed me. She kept looking at me like I was just a friend. If she finally opened her eyes and saw what was right in front of her...we could have had something pretty damn amazing."

I didn't have a clue whom he was talking about. "What happened to her?"

He shrugged and never answered.

Rex opened the door and walked inside. "Yo, it's me."

"We know," Zeke said. "Who else would just walk in like that?"

"Or because you knew I was coming." He came into the living room and stood by the back of the couch.

"What did you need to do?" I asked.

Rex held up a Hallmark card. "I got you guys something." He handed it over. "Keep in mind, I'm penniless right now."

Zeke took it then turned it over as he examined it. "What's it for?"

Rex put his hands in his pockets. "You know...for everything."

Zeke looked at me before he did the honors and opened the card. Then he moved beside me on the couch so we both could read it at the same time. It was a red card with a bunch of pink hearts everywhere.

"I know the card is kind of lame..." Rex shrugged and looked at the ground.

Zeke and Rae,

I just wanted to say thank you for everything you've done for me. You weren't obligated to do anything, and I didn't ask for anything, but you wanted to help anyway. I'd be drowning right now if it weren't for the both of you. I may be broke and without a cent to my name, but I feel rich having the two of you in my life.

Sincerely,
Rex

"Awe…" It was one of the sweetest things Rex had ever done.

"That was thoughtful," Zeke said. "Thanks, man." He left the couch then hugged Rex. They didn't usually show affection to each other, but this was an exception. He clapped him on the shoulder. "You would do it for me."

Rex nodded.

I came around the couch and stopped in front of him. "You know I would do anything for you, Rex. You took care of me when it wasn't your responsibility, and I'll always take care of you."

Rex didn't handle emotion very well, so he looked uncomfortable. "I know. You have no idea how thankful I am that we have each other…even if we don't have anyone else."

I opened my arms. "Should we hug or something?"

The corner of his lip lifted in a half smile. "I guess we can...but we can't let this turn into a habit."

"Deal." I pulled him in for a hug and wrapped my arms around his waist.

Rex rested his chin on my head. His arms were around my shoulders.

Zeke stood there silently, giving us a moment.

Rex cleared his throat and stepped away. "Okay, enough of the lovey-dovey shit." He crossed his arms over his chest and didn't look at me again. "I need a beer or something."

Zeke chuckled. "Or maybe a shot?"

"Yeah." Rex snapped his fingers. "I need a shot of vodka."

"Coming right up." Zeke headed into the kitchen.

I kept smiling at Rex because I knew he was a big softy under that rough exterior.

"What?"

I shrugged. "Nothing."

"You're giving me that look."

"What look?" I played innocent.

"Like you're thinking or something."

"Well, I do think pretty often."

"Well, I don't like it."

I gave him a playful slap on the arm. "You really want to know what I was thinking?"

"Not really."

I crossed my arms over my chest.

"Okay, I already know what you were thinking."

"What?"

"That you love me." He cringed like he was disgusted by his own words.

I grinned from ear-to-ear. "You're a mind reader. And I know what you're thinking too."

"Do not," he snapped.

"You love me too."

He rolled his eyes and walked away.

"What?" I said. "You do."

"Don't push it." He walked into the kitchen and his voice carried. "Zeke, where the hell is that goddamn shot?"

Ray of Light

The story continues in Book 2, Ray of Hope.

Dear Reader,

Thank you for reading Ray of Light. I hope you enjoyed reading it as much as I enjoyed writing it. If you could leave a short review, it would help me so much! Those reviews are the best kind of support you can give an author. Thank you!

Wishing you love,

E. L. Todd

Want To Stalk Me?

Subscribe to my newsletter for updates on new releases, giveaways, and for my comical monthly newsletter. You'll get all the dirt you need to know. Sign up today.

www.eltoddbooks.com

Facebook:

https://www.facebook.com/ELTodd42

Twitter:

@E_L_Todd

Now you have no reason not to stalk me. You better get on that.

EL's Elites

I know I'm lucky enough to have super fans, you know, the kind that would dive off a cliff for you. They have my back through and through. They love my books, and they love spreading the word. Their biggest goal is to see me on the New York Times bestsellers list, and they'll stop at nothing to make it happen. While it's a lot of work, it's also a lot of fun. What better way to make friendships than to connect with people who love the same thing you do?

Are you one of these super fans?

If so, send a request to join the Facebook group. It's closed, so you'll have a hard time finding it without the link. Here it is:

https://www.facebook.com/groups/119232 6920784373

Hope to see you there, ELITE!

KNIGHT MEMORIAL LIBRARY